THE MIRROR MEN

THE MIRROR MEN

P. R. BROWN

By the same author:

The Gods of Our Time
Dreams and Illusions Revisited
The Mountain Dwellers

First Published in Great Britain in 2018 by DB Publishing,
an imprint of JMD Media Ltd

ISBN 9781780915722

Printed and bound in the UK

1

And the Walls Came Tumbling Down

Leaning on his walking-stick, Frank Russell stared at the rubble, with a look as forlorn and downcast as that on the faces of Captain Scott and his party in that famous photograph (or 'selfie', in current jargon) taken at the South Pole, when Scott and company had been beaten to the post and now faced a thousand-mile trek on a return journey that would prove fatal to them all.

Frank mused with a mixture of disdain and nostalgia. They had not even had the decency to pull The Red Lion down brick by brick, with the care that had been taken to build it. Bulldozers are devoid of respect, and a death sentence had hung over the old place for long enough, ever since pubs in general were hailed as 'dens of iniquity' by the moral denizens of society, who had themselves grown both in numbers and in aggressive evangelism. Pubs might have enjoyed a reprieve had the soft drinks alternative caught on; since it hadn't, they were doomed to economic decline and an inevitable demise, and The Red Lion had silently waited its turn with the humility of the lamb.

What had once been the site of a cosy retreat from the insanities of life now resembled a bomb site. *What would Henry and Percy say?* thought Frank, as he feebly kicked a piece of rubble against a dented beer can. He knew what they would say. Probably nothing. They would simply stand staring just as he was and let the weather say it all: the skies were grey and fine rain fell, as a fitting gesture of condolence, and a peal of distant thunder seemed to add condemnation.

Who would have thought it? – that it would come to this? Actually, Frank, Henry Westwood and Percy Fletcher had all thought it; but it had always been a question of expecting the worst and hoping for the best. Now the worst had happened, and Henry and Percy were not here to see it, fortunately for them, if fortune can ever be attributed to the cruel, eternal absence of old friends, cruel because eternal, and not just old friends but kindred spirits and birds of a feather. Frank called to mind one of Percy's favourite aphorisms, or what Percy himself took to be an axiomatic piece of wisdom: *The first and principal tragedy of life is death; the second is the failure to understand the first.* Percy was nothing if not articulate, a skill derived from wide reading and self-study. He could turn his hand to any style and to every occasion; anything, in fact, from the measured aphorisms he was wont to produce in The Red Lion to the occasional letter of complaint written to the local authority, usually on behalf of the elderly or less able, concerning such profound conundrums as potholes in the road or the persistent shortcomings of public transport. Percy was an all-rounder, alright. But he was at his best when complaining to the Highest Authority of all. If a new arrival had been mentioned in casual conversation, he would be ready with his characteristic input: *All new life begins with at least a modicum of hope – yet all new life is, in its very nature, tragedy in the making. Oh, Lord!* Percy's wisdom, enunciated as though reading out loud from profound texts, rarely met with any response, apart from a slight pause and a slurp of beer all round. After all, Percy was a hard act to follow, and neither Frank nor Henry was ever in a mood to attempt the Olympian task, even if they could.

Yes, but who would have thought it? Frank, Henry and Percy met every week in The Red Lion, regular as Swiss clockwork, and they always sat at the same table in the same dingy corner, adjacent to a window that was rarely cleaned – not that it was worth looking out of it, even in broad daylight, for the grey and grimy terraced houses opposite had little to offer those with artistic discernment. Such sights were common in northern towns, places still clinging to the thick coarse apron strings of the Industrial Revolution. The terraced houses remained; but The Red Lion was no more. The galling thing is that The Red Lion was the nearest retreat from the ugliness of all this grey and grimy architecture; the ugliness remained, the retreat had gone. Now, what was it Percy had said about ugliness? *When Beauty walks in the door, laughter stops; when Ugliness enters, it begins* – or something like that. Trouble is, memory's such a trickster, fools us all and always has his way despite our very best efforts. Things should have been written down – but that would've seemed over the top, if not a species of mockery, at the time, and might have given old Percy more airs and graces than even he deserved.

Every Friday they would meet, in that same dingy corner, and, after the preliminary debate about whose round it was, they would settle down to what the majority, on this planet at least, would regard as an equally dingy evening. Though it would be unfair to give the impression that all such evenings were devoid of memorable moments. Henry was very much one for keeping things to himself, for keeping his cards close to his chest, but one evening in particular would remain with him for the rest of his life. It was an evening on which he fell instantly in love and never to fall out of it. He was a bachelor and lived alone, and, then in his fifties, had long abandoned the romantic notions of his youth. But on that particularly evening, his settled way of life with all its assumptions was about to receive a blow from which it would never recover. For in walked a woman, perhaps in her thirties, accompanied by a tall well-dressed fellow to whom Henry took an instant and unshakeable dislike; she appeared to Henry as close to a long-lost love as he could ever get, the soulmate for whom he might have spent his whole life searching. Such feelings were, of course, the result of pure conjecture and were based entirely upon what Henry considered to be her striking good looks: she was a brunette, of medium height and slim build; and, as far as he could make out, with eyes black as a starless night in the depths of the Yorkshire moors and just as mysterious, though he could not possibly have been close enough to confirm it; and rather sallow skin, dressed in such a way as to reveal not too much and not too little, the kind of modesty which Henry found strangely seductive. For Henry, she was the feminine ideal, the paradigm of femininity he had dreamed about in his youth, a dream that had become lost in the numerous folds and twists and turns of stultifying routine and grim long-term resignation and abandoned hope. Now that dream had suddenly and unexpectedly come rushing back, a crushing bolt out of nowhere, and distinctly barbed, for all he could do was watch, without being seen to watch, and muse, without forgetting to sip his beer – he was obliged to 'act normal' in the most abnormal of circumstances. Outwardly, at least, the misery was short-lived, for her wholly reprehensible companion decided that it would be better to get on their way, for it was later than he had thought, he was heard to say, and they both left. Henry watched them go, with a mixture of relief and devastation. He continued to sip his beer and exchange nods with Percy and Frank, though he had no idea what the subject of the conversation was and could not have cared less. It had been a defining moment, a kind of crossroads in his life, though what it defined and which road he should now take was a total mystery; all he knew, or, rather, all he *felt*, was that nothing would or could ever be the same again. It was as momentous as the conversion on the Road to Damascus, except that he was neither converted nor on the road to Damascus, or on any road at all for that matter.

One did not need to go as far afield as Damascus to find parallels with the unforgettable incident in the pub. Henry had had a similar life-changing experience as a schoolboy in his teens, when he was besotted with a female classmate who, one might not be surprised to know, shared essential features with the girl in the pub: both had about them, at least in Henry's eyes, the magical allure of a gypsy maiden, dark and mysterious, yet warm and inviting. All he needed was sufficient courage to ask her out, but fear of rejection held him back. Not even courage of the Dutch variety, in the form of the equivalent of a glass of wine smuggled to him by a sympathetic classmate, proved efficacious. Henry simply sat at the back of the classroom in a mild stupor, unable to make the first move, or indeed any move at all. He subsequently stalked the girl with his mind, and hoped against all hope to catch sight of her, perhaps on a bus as it happened to pass in the vague direction of the nearby village in which she lived; but he never did – and then her parents moved away, and poor Henry began to consider her as a lost love; and it was just like him to fail to acknowledge it was a lost opportunity, for he could never bring himself to face the unpalatable truth that he had been incapable of trying his luck, of taking a risk for the sake of love. If, of course, love is what it was, and not simply the infatuation that we normally associate with youth. Call it love, if you like, or call it infatuation.

No matter; whatever it was, it was not of short duration but dogged him for years, and, as far as we know, might have dogged him his whole life through, as ill-health often dogs the lives of the gifted. The memory of the girl in the pub joined ranks with the memory of the girl in the classroom, and the very best that could be said of both memories is that they were bitter-sweet. But, on balance, more bitter than sweet. Henry knew very well that one can get uncomfortably close to one's past, not necessarily because the past is a narrative of tragedy, but because the past is dead and cannot be revived, and because the past is of another, now alien, world. Better, then, to keep evocations of the past, sights and sounds and smells, buried too deep to sense, too vague to recall, all wrapped up snugly in coffins of lead where they can do the least harm, and where they are impervious to the light of day. But sometimes they creep out and catch us unawares, when we are least able to deal with them without hurt. It is also therefore incidents, like the one in the pub, and not merely memories, that are bitter-sweet. Perhaps he imagined that a second chance had turned up in the pub that evening; that Fate had forgiven him for his youthful failings. Or did he think he was still being punished? Or was it an intoxicating mixture of both? We shall never know. For now Henry is incapable of being asked. And if he were still among the living, it is doubtful whether the matter could be settled in his own mind.

One thing is certain: Henry did not, and never could, actively subscribe to the dictum that Faint Heart Never Won Fair Lady. He was a born observer, even of his own fate. He was an extra-terrestrial spectator of a world he could never quite comprehend.

Frank, Henry and Percy were, one might say, birds of a feather. Between them beer and opinions flowed with ever-increasing fluidity and ever-decreasing validity until the nights wore on and the pennies wore out. The mutual attraction between them consisted in something they shared in common. Perhaps it is this recognition of a common element that draws us to another, like a magnet. And recognising this common element might be the result of observing something about someone that sets him or her apart from others. In a crowded room, for example, the way someone talks, moves, walks, or even what they wear, may suggest to us that they are someone we would like to know, for what we observe is an indication of that common element, evidence for believing that it exists, and so we like to conclude that it is a pointer to something in someone that we would like to know better. We may be right, and we may be wrong; but it is an instinctive thing, which is perhaps why it is so entertaining, and often instructive, to watch others in a crowded room, as though on a voyage of hopeful discovery. Or it might be simply a word or gesture that sparks one's interest, as the word 'sufficient' sparked Percy's; for it reminded him of his father, deceased for almost half a century, for whom excess was a vice; Percy's father was the embodiment of moderation, no second helpings for him. 'You should leave the table feeling you can eat just as much again' was his watch-phrase; so, asked if he would care for a second helping, he would simply reply, 'No, that was sufficient thank you.' Percy idealised his father, and if this were the only example one needed to consider, one might be tempted to say that a man is good if he recognises goodness in another; but such platitudes, like memory, are dubious aids to judgement.

Therefore, let us simply say that Frank, Henry and Percy were birds of a feather. But we feel constrained to inquire what *kind* of feather they were all birds of!

Not birds of prey, one would say, let alone Golden Eagles, which soar so high and swoop so low, adorning the skies with their unrivalled majesty, brooking no hindrance, impervious to either praise or condemnation.

2
Intimations of Fear

The walls may have tumbled down. But they were nowhere near Jericho – or so our three friends had always thought. What could a northern English town possibly have in common with that ancient city? The comparison was absurd.

Yet, one thing is related to another, and sometimes in ways we would never suspect. Which brings us once again to our search for the common element that governed the fellowship in The Red Lion.

Take Frank, for example. People are wont to say that the world is small and getting smaller, and many would consider this a very fine thing. But it is by no means a truth that Frank greeted with much enthusiasm, and, given a choice, it is one he would have preferred not to greet at all. Frank's own world was in a continual state of reduction. He now lived in a small third-floor council flat, having moved from a semi-detached house which he could no longer afford to run; and inside the flat he had, by slow degrees, emigrated to the bedroom where even his armchair resided in stately partnership, so that the two-bedroomed apartment now, for all practical purposes, consisted of bedroom, kitchen and washroom, the living room and second bedroom hardly ever used at all. The fairly spacious garden he had once enjoyed was replaced by a postage stamp to the rear.

And, although an avid reader of travel books, Frank was averse to the idea of travelling anywhere that did not *demand* to be travelled to. It will come as no great surprise, therefore, that for all his talk and speculation and deliberation concerning the most suitable pair of binoculars to purchase, they were to be employed not on his travels, but merely for watching the birds that pecked at the humble greenery on the postage stamp of the ground-floor garden. Frank, seated in his armchair, would watch the birds, from his third-floor bedroom window, as they pecked here and there. Why or how he felt entertained by this passive activity is hard to determine. Suffice to say that the binoculars he had purchased with such gravity of conviction and with such an eye to achieving the very best for the very best price were put to the most modest use imaginable.

Modest use is not necessarily without incident. On one of those occasions when Frank was watching birds hop and peck, and peck and hop, he noticed a large bird, which he was meticulous enough to identify as a hooded crow, which simply sat in the grass of that postage stamp, seeming to stare ahead of itself as though hypnotised. Frank watched through his brand-new, not-overly-expensive but not-overly-cheap binoculars, expecting some sign of life; when it eventually came, the bird seemed to crawl through the grass, its right wing somewhat limp and lifeless; it stopped again, transfixed; Frank continued to watch, correctly drawing the conclusion that the poor bird had seen better days and was now experiencing the last of them. Frank himself was transfixed, with only the occasional blink to suggest life, and drew the further conclusion that it was the black cat from next door that was the author of the foul deed. He had never liked that cat, principally because it was black, and because he had the notion that if one passed a black cat the day would go well, and if the cat passed you it would go badly. Frank had spent many a morning standing in the doorway for signs of the creature, hoping to cross its path before it could cross his; it became a kind of cat-and-mouse game, with Frank adopting the role of the mouse; except that it was not really a game but something that Frank took at any rate half seriously, and anything that one takes half seriously is never wholly a game, for the more seriously one takes it the less fun it becomes.

But the question of establishing the culprit after the fact was far less important than the question of dealing with the fact itself; the question being: what now is to be done, not about the cat, but about the poor bird. These thoughts ran through Frank's mind as he blinked and stared, stared and blinked. Clearly the poor creature's fellow crows were disinclined to do anything about it. Frank managed to drag his gaze away from the victim sufficiently long to see crows perched on tall trees in the nearest corner of the school playing field that bordered the postage stamp. There they were, looking as regal as you like, but doing nothing at all, though they must have seen the plight one of their number was in far below. But what could they possibly do, anyway. They could hardly swoop down and take the poor thing away in their talons to provide either hospitalisation or at least a more dignified place to die. Frank knew such thoughts were ridiculous; but he could find nothing in them to smile at, let alone joke about; and he knew that if he related them to Henry and Percy they would regard it as incontrovertible evidence of dementia, and they wouldn't be smiling, either.

No, there was no getting away from it. The solution, insofar as one could speak of a solution, was squarely in Frank's hands and no one else's. But what exactly was he to do? He knew that people who shoot birds, either for their stomachs or, more commonly, for their egos, were not at all averse to stamping on the heads of wounded birds, ostensibly to put them out of their misery. No, that was unthinkable. Frank could not possibly bring himself to do such a thing. In any case, the bird would need to remain quite still while Frank approached to deliver the *coup de grace*; the likelihood is that the bird would not allow Frank to approach and would scuttle here, there and everywhere. No, no, no, that was not feasible.

After an hour or so of watching and blinking – with Frank all the while hoping against hope that a miracle might occur and that suddenly the bird would somehow regain its composure and fly off to live a long and fruitful life, as though the creature had been fooling all along, perhaps unable to fly off and lose all the attention it craved, like a spoiled child or a diva of mediocrity – after an hour or so, and perhaps a good deal more, the thought struck Frank that he might phone a vet and get the vet to handle matters. Dragging himself away from the scene, he consulted the Yellow Pages and phoned a local vet, forgetting that it was Saturday and that he would be most unlikely to get an answer. In fact, his call was answered by the receptionist. No vet was available to come to the rescue, but the suggestion was that Frank should take the creature to the vet, preferably in a box, a shoebox, or preferably something a little larger, and the vet would himself perform the *coup de grace.*

Oh dear. Frank ended the phone call with a thank you and an I'll-do-my-best. But, really, this suggestion was hardly much better than his delivering the *coup de grace* himself. He imagined approaching the bird with a box – did he *have* a box, anyway? – and the bird fluttering like mad and hoping every which way and not allowing Frank to get anywhere near enough to plonk the box over it; and then, of course, there was the trip to the vet's, which would have to be taken by car. No, but the worst part was getting close enough to the poor creature without giving it a heart attack, not to mention Frank's own cardiac responses. No, no, no – the whole thing bristled with difficulties. Fairly bristled!

So much so that Frank decided to do what was up to that point virtually impossible – to put down his binoculars, get up out of his armchair, go to the kitchen and make himself a cup of tea; moreover, he was able to bring himself to supervise the kettle while it boiled, ignoring, if not unconsciously relishing in, the proverb that a watched kettle never boils.

This done, he returned to his armchair, placed his tea close by, picked up his binoculars, stared out of the window to locate the bird. The creature must have changed its position on the postage stamp; Frank looked around, but no, he could not find it, and, after adjusting his binoculars like a captain at sea and at war, finally concluded, with a relief so intense that he preferred not to acknowledge it even to himself, that it had hopped or crawled, not to say been taken off by the dreaded black cat, through the hedges to another garden, and perhaps into the playing fields beyond – to a place, anyway, far beyond Henry's sphere of responsibility, like a well-intentioned sheriff in the Old West who suddenly finds himself outside his own jurisdiction and therefore unable to pursue either the good or the bad or the ugly.

To all intents and purposes, the case was closed. Frank was unspeakably relieved. On the other hand, he went to bed that night with a conscience as deep and as wide as the Grand Canyon. It had been an incident that he would never forget, and that would never forget him. It was an incident that had become a memory as soon as passed, and one that was very much fit for a coffin of lead.

Frank's interest in birds never diminished, of course. He continued to watch with as much interest as ever. Early mornings were best. After all, what better way to begin the days of one's retirement than to gaze through one's binoculars on the wonders of nature and nature's creatures? The beauty of retirement was that it allowed one to gaze at leisure, or indeed gaze at all, unlike the world of work, which chained you to a desk and a routine not of your own making. Free at last, Frank could gaze to his heart's content and philosophise on his gazing. There were, for example, what he liked to call the Guardians of the rooftops and the chimney pots and the trees and the telegraph poles. Now, what were they? Crows, yes, but what sort? Or, perhaps they were rooks. Frank never managed to tell them clearly apart, though he had bought a book which claimed to help him to do so; never mind, his failure to distinguish different species was also something that deserved a place in the coffin of lead; it was splitting hairs, anyway, or rather splitting feathers; a crow is a crow, after all; Frank preferred to blame his eyesight, which naturally was not what it used to be. And so, he was happy to conclude that a crow is a crow – unless, of course, it was a rook – but he had scratched his head long enough about that. Magpies, thankfully, presented no such challenges. He was quite comfortable about magpies. But the thought that really put to rest his own sense of failing was that, after all, they were all – crows, hooded, grey and otherwise, rooks and magpies – they were all members of the *same family*! And what he really dreamed of observing was a raven, being attracted to the creature after reading Poe's dark poem, but, no matter, for he could never be sure that what he was seeing was a raven or a crow, of whatever variety, or even a particularly large rook. He was content, therefore, to dream of one day seeing a raven, whether or not he knew that what he was seeing was a raven or a crow incognito – a crow in raven's feathers, so to speak. The thought had struck him that he might see ravens if he were to visit the Tower of London; but the train journey and the subsequent and inevitable queuing put him off; he would no doubt get round to it – though, of course, he never did. Frank did not consider himself to be a seasoned traveller – and it was too late to aspire to being so; and the argument that the Tower of London was little more than a two-hour journey, with a simple change *en route*, did not strike him as sufficiently compelling.

Frank therefore continued to make out the Guardians from his bedroom window, every day, like clockwork.

3
A Parliament of Crows

When Frank was about to go to the expense of buying the best pair of binoculars his money could stretch to, he had invited the opinions of Henry and Percy, neither of whom knew the first thing about such matters, let alone optics. (Indeed, the very word 'optics' would require dictionary investigation, if only to rule out the possibility that it might denote something offensive.)

But the whole business of observing Frank's Guardians was of immense interest to Percy. Frank might philosophise on these rooftop, treetop scenes, but Percy, whose life seemed to be a narrative neatly punctuated by one aphorism after another, was far better at summing up Frank's findings, much better at enunciating platitudes. He was the man to go to should one wish for the ideal mixture of wisdom and brevity. He was delighted to muse on the chattering of these intelligent birds in the early morning dew and suggested that these birds, as much if not more than any other family of birds, deserved the title *parliament*. They were not merely of the same family, but honourable members of the same democratic institution; at least, it appeared to be democratic on account of the fact that no one bird appeared to dominate the discussion. All chattered away, sometimes all at once, in tongues incomprehensible, presumably on the subject of the state of their Union, a world we could never ourselves know but which was very much dependent on our own. Their 'Kaaaw! Kaaaw!' sounded like a gruff 'Whaaat! Whaaat!' which might suggest either that they were hard of hearing or were simply and profoundly discontent with the mess in which they found themselves and were bitterly lamenting the hegemony of the world of men.

'They are a reflection of ourselves!' blurted Percy, after clearing his throat with a particularly large swallow, and finally achieving his aphoristic contribution to the whole subject.

'Mankind,' mumbled Frank, with a knowing nod.

'No. *Us*!'

Frank gave him a quizzical look.

'Us, here. Like us,' Percy reiterated, his eyes darting from Frank to Henry and back again. 'Like us,' he added, his intonation dropping, in a rather solemn, downcast tone.

Henry, with slightly raised eyebrows, peered over the rim of his glass.

No more was said. Glasses were drained, and another round debated and settled.

Well, perhaps there was something in what Percy said. It needed some thinking about – or, perhaps not. Perhaps these three men were in the world without being a part of it; perhaps they were cocooned in their own little parliament, if that's what Percy meant. Were they ever part of the world in which they found themselves? No doubt they had been – in their youth, years ago, long before their youth had taken flight, before dreams had faded and the whole world had become foreign and far less palatable. If this is what the crows were babbling about, they had a point. But at least it could be said that their humanity had matured, as wine is said to mature; for lamentation, complaint and critique must have a subject as well as an object; you cannot complain about what is bad unless at least a part of you is good. And there was much to complain about.

Yes, but who would have thought it? Who would have thought that behind those walls, the walls of The Red Lion, men sat and spoke and lamented, and that those walls were now pulled down? – pulled down, not to allow for renovation or rebuilding, but pulled down forever.

And to think that this was done under a pretext that, in their youth, had been unthinkable and of historical interest only!

With the kind of intolerable irony with which most of us are all too familiar, Henry had adopted a cliché from Percy's abundant stock. Henry would say, 'It's a question of priorities,' a phrase which he would throw into a conversation whenever he deemed it appropriate to do so, and even on occasions when he did not (just for fun). That Henry should take a liking to this cliché was ironic in view of the fact that his own life would appear to many to suggest that he knew as much about his own priorities as he did about astrophysics. No matter. For it seemed now that priorities had certainly changed. Of this, the destruction of The Red Lion was abundant proof.

On the question of common elements, it must be said that Percy, like Frank, had never been one for travelling far afield. The air of much-travelled wisdom which his aphorisms and platitudes might suggest to a casual observer were not the result of geographical exploration and diverse cultural experience. Indeed, with physical movement, however far and wide, he was not overly impressed. Which perhaps helps explain why he had never taken much of an interest in sport, a whole dimension of life which held for him no particular interest, let alone thrills. That a grown man, or for that matter woman, should don a scarf in support of a football team and plod to a stadium, let alone a stadium in another town, let alone a stadium in another country, to watch a game of football – this was quite beyond him. Mind you, he had always made out to others that his lack of interest was due to a kind of self-preservation, in that he was frightened of becoming too interested in anything lest it took over his whole life by becoming an unjustifiable obsession; at least, this is how he attempted to deal with stares of disbelief whenever asked a question like, 'Which team do *you* support?' and answered, 'Well, none, actually.'

Percy's dislike of movement was shared by Frank. But this is not to say that his platitudes and aphorisms were merely plucked from the air, rootless and depersonalised. On the contrary, Percy was as much an observer as Frank, but the object of his gaze was not birds, but people, who then became the subject of his musings. Besides he was very well read. Indeed, like John Keats he could almost equally claim to be 'Much travelled in the realms of gold', to have seen many 'goodly states and kingdoms' and to have rounded 'many western islands' which 'bards in fealty to Apollo hold'. For his travels were literary and his musings cerebral. And to those who believe that a man must travel widely and meet half the world before he can justify a claim to wisdom, it must be said that many an Old Salt and seasoned traveller has ended his weary days with no more wisdom or comprehension than when he started out, and there may be many who have rather less. Nor is this observation as barbed as it may appear. One may recall the joke made by Sir Arthur Eddington, the so-called but yet underrated Father of Modern Astrophysics, that in 1932 he knew all about the composition of the sun, in 1934 rather less, and in 1936 nothing at all. The complications and nuances of knowledge and experience are such that of human beings as well as the heavenly bodies, one might fairly claim that to know more is to know less. A paradox that we shall not pursue, and that Percy would not wish to pursue. Suffice to say that those who make it their business to be much-travelled are not necessarily at an advantage when it comes to worldly wisdom; just as a priest is not necessarily the best source of moral advice.

In short, Percy was a thinker, not a doer. Even in his youth his mother had complained, in one of her not infrequent *the-trouble-with-you* outbursts, that he might be far better off thinking less and just getting on with it, though getting on with precisely *what* she consistently failed to specify. Perhaps she was thinking of those rare occasions when

Percy could be induced to hang a picture on the wall, for his heart was never in DIY. Fixing a picture hook would be accompanied by many a muffled blasphemy, many a devilish imprecation, or peppering of unflattering remarks against the ancestry of anyone who had requested the job to be done. If by some unsavoury magic the picture hook could have fixed itself to the wall, Percy would have dabbled in the black arts to get it done. As it was, he tended to do a less than perfect job of it while at the same time causing himself incommensurate misery; as though doing a bad job might release him from obligations to accede to future DIY requests – if so, let it be here recorded that such releases singularly failed to materialise.

The common element, the bond that held these three men together, was, however, deep, as distinct from surface personality traits. If their humanity had matured with age, it had also owed a great deal to their wives, who were all now deceased and by all three were considered to have been, unquestionably, indisputably, their better halves. Grief and a profound sense of loss, shared by all three men, bound them together, much as an attack by an overwhelming force might cause soldiers to bunch together for mutual protection and survival. Their bond was therefore instinctive rather than acquired through gradual familiarity and was, perhaps, for this reason deeper and more unshakeable. The devotion and gratitude each felt towards his wife bound them together, as though in a common cause, to keep the memory of their wives alive and well and powerful still; the only thing they could do, for they could not bring them back. Henry had told them how like a small child he had felt without his wife, a small child lost in a huge supermarket, not knowing which way to turn. Their company and mutual grieving seemed to save him from total oblivion.

Time is said to be a great healer. But when people who suffer the loss of a lifetime companion have, themselves, relatively few years left, and nothing in particular to occupy them, time is not so efficacious. Time itself requires time. 'Dai tempo al tempo,' as the Italians have it. And if Time has little chance, then we must help each other all the more. Which is what each of these three men felt, even if the thought were never articulated. Indeed, to articulate the thought might have degraded it.

They needed each other and were thrown together by the excessive tragedy of life: death. They were all retired when first they met: Henry had been an accountant; Percy, a history teacher in a large comprehensive, and Frank a landscape gardener. Like most people fortunate enough to survive the world of work and unlucky enough to have to tolerate the solitude of retirement, they seldom talked about their working lives, rather like soldiers who survive the hell of war and are reluctant to go back there even in memory, or like former prison inmates who would rather look forward than back – forward to new and unblemished pastures or forward to another, and more successful, perpetration of crime. Percy had grown old in his job, and the older he became the greater was the distance between himself and those he attempted, too often in vain, to enlighten; for as long as he could he functioned as a kind of intermediary between past and future, between the past which was his, and the future that belonged to those he struggled to teach, until, finally, he was obliged to bow out, with a handshake here and there and a few 'Happy Retirement' cards to plant on his bookshelf in commemoration of the grand, but to everyone else eminently forgettable, event. For Frank, gardening had become physically intolerable, and his spade had at last surrendered to a hip replacement; retirement age and hip-replacement had happily dovetailed into one another in an act of superb timing. And as for Henry, accountancy had never held him spellbound; it had simply paid the mortgage. His failing eyesight had in any case put paid to any suggestion that he should continue beyond retirement age.

So, these three superannuated gentlemen would simply sit, relaxed in each other's company, until something 'came up' in the news that they deemed worthy of comment, of praise or of criticism. And, of course, something was sure to come up on a daily basis.

And the kind of stuff coming up in recent times had merited their closest scrutiny, for it was of unprecedented concern. Well, not quite unprecedented. In fact, not unprecedented at all. Not if one knew what Percy knew.

4

The Lord's Power Went Over the Nation

Who would have thought it? The old Red Lion, now nothing more than a scattered heap of rubble. As Frank looked on he remembered what Percy had said about empty classrooms. 'There's nothing more depressing than an empty classroom,' he had said, 'I mean on the last day of term when all the kids have gone home, and you're there collecting up your bits of paper and you're stuffing things into your briefcase; you pause, you look round and … well, it's empty and its quiet. You think, 'Things aren't as they should be.' And if you walk round the school all you sense is an empty shell, and you know the place wasn't meant to be like that. So sad. So depressing. You know what I mean?' Henry and Frank had nodded over their pints, though they hadn't known it as Percy had known it. But as Frank looked on that pile of rubble that was once their mutual retreat and the seat of their shared reflections, he knew what Percy had meant. What had once been their mutual haven was now a gap between two sets of terraced houses, a space, a nothingness enveloped in grey and red brick on either side and topped with a grey sky which continued to rain down on Frank's head, as though shedding tears of sympathy for an incomprehensible loss. So Frank thought.

Which called to mind another loss, that of Sally, his better half. Sal had been a bundle of fun, but she wouldn't have laughed at this. She had a relentless sense of fun, but this was mixed with biting commentaries on anything, usually of a broadly political or religious nature, that might upset her. Her appearance would have suggested the fun, but not the seriousness that intermixed with it. Being short, very plump, with a waist that might have encircled a minor planet, frizzy ginger hair which stuck out each side of her head in points, she resembled a circus clown who was just about to don the customary make-up before entering the ring with a handful of custard pies. But this was a calling she could never have taken up, even if she had wanted to, since circuses had been outlawed years before in the name of animal rights. No, her clowning was confined to talking non-stop about any issue that had temporarily caught her imagination, like the cost of bus travel to and from the city centre, and pausing only to register a nod of humble acquiescence from anyone unfortunate enough to be in the vicinity. Throughout her tirades, however, she rarely ceased to smile, and would terminate her invective with a wave of the hand and some such phrase as, 'Well, anyway, that's how it is!' as though, by merely throwing abuse at some issue, she had succeeded in resolving it.

Poor Sal. Poor Frank! Frank missed her so much that some mornings he could hardly stir from his bed. What he would give to hear Sal again in one of her tirades! He suspected that his concern for the disabled crow he had watched through his binoculars was a replay of how he had suffered to watch Sal's decline and her descent into nothingness. He had been helpless to stop or reverse it; just as helpless as he had felt while watching the crow.

Yes, but what would she say now? He could hear her quite clearly deep and indelible inside his head: 'Well, I could've told you that! Look, it's like gardening – and by the way, when are you going to make those herb boxes? – it's like gardening – you turn your back for five minutes and the weeds are everywhere. It's like that – it's just like that …' Her voice faded from his head. Sal was not there, not there to see the rubble that was once The Red Lion. Frank was alone and had to think his own thoughts. The loss of their wives had given Frank, Henry and Percy a sad form of liberation in that there was nothing more they could do to help them, and each had only himself to worry about. If this is a kind of liberation, is there any sadder? But as if to add oil to an already insatiable fire, Frank had lost Henry and Percy, too.

Percy would have agreed with Sal that it was just like that – that it was just like a garden neglected. Turn your back on human beings and you never know what they might get up to next. And that is precisely what had happened. The insidious growth of weeds was something you could verify by occasional observation. Frank remembered the history lesson that Percy gave them in The Red Lion, and he was beginning to understand that 'Yes, it was just like that!' Percy's voice seemed to boom from his grave. And Sal was quick to say her piece, 'I could've told you!'

'Sedition,' Percy had mumbled, one night in The Red Lion in what now seemed a long time ago.

'I take my hat off to you,' said Henry, 'you come out with the weirdest things.'

'Thinking aloud. And don't talk to me about *hats*!' Percy rounded.

'Well, come out with it, then!' Frank put in.

'The Quakers. George Fox. Seventeenth century. Heard of him?'

'No,' said Frank.

'No,' said Henry, 'but I'm sure we're about to.'

'Well, it's a good example how things can start.'

It was all coming back, as Frank started to wind his weary way back home through the fine rain, which now fell like mist. He was taking his time. His hip, the one they had not replaced, was playing up, as it always did in spells of cold humidity; besides, there was no one to go home to. He remembered Percy's anecdote about hats. George Fox's friend had been imprisoned for refusing to take his hat off in church. When Percy related the story, Frank had regarded it as no more than an anecdote – an amusing tale, perhaps not altogether true, perhaps not true at all and, if true, something that belonged to the past and its primitive thinking. Just how much credence to give it was not an item in his consideration – it would only put them off their beer, a rather silly alternative to doing nothing and saying nothing. But Percy had regarded it as absolutely true, for it had been related by George Fox himself in his *Journal,* and, whatever one thought of Fox's religion, Fox himself could never be considered a teller of tall tales. According to Percy, Fox objected to his friend's arrest on the grounds that the presiding priest wore two caps in church, one white and one black – both caps, Fox pointed out, were brimless – but, he reasoned, given that the brim on his friend's hat was merely there to protect the wearer's neck from the rain, there should be no reasonable objection against the wearing of hats with brims, in church or out. The governor of the prison then objected that these were frivolous matters, causing Fox to counter that if they were frivolous, then how could such frivolities justify his friend's imprisonment? At this the governor was enraged and threatened to lock Fox up, too. However, Fox managed to convince him that such rage and threats were unchristian things, pointing out that Christ and his disciples never imprisoned anyone. The governor relented, Fox's friend was released, and Fox was invited to dine at the governor's house. All ended very well, everything due, as Fox put it, to the *Power of the Lord,* the sort of phrase which he was wont to employ when things went his way.

After relaying this little narrative to Sal, who, uncharacteristically, had listened in silence long enough to understand it, she declared, with a wave of the hand and a throwing back of the head: 'Well, small things may have big endings!' by which she presumably meant that a trivial thing might well land you in jail; Frank was content with presumption, since Sal's announcement never had the benefit of further clarification, and he would never have dared to request it.

But there was a further presumption that Frank was not entitled to make, namely that history could never possibly embarrass itself by repeating the errors of trivia. He needed to acknowledge that although there was indeed such a thing as 'moving on', when a wave beaches itself on the shoreline it will invariably bring with it flotsam and jetsam, very rarely mermaids and Spanish treasure. Time may move forward and many assumptions may be proved false or be otherwise dropped and many good things may take their place, but since human nature does not improve in leaps and bounds, one can also expect baggage of a less welcome kind. The proverbial leopard and human nature are assailed by the same reluctance to abandon the primitive and embrace the simple light of day. If only the crows on the rooftops could speak they might have told him as much – which is why they resented the hegemony of mankind.

Sal was indubitably right. Small beginnings may have big ends, and the distance between the small and the big may be short; therefore the intermediary steps might go unnoticed, until too late.

To say that the power of the Lord went over the nation is a small step to a possibly unwieldy conclusion, a conclusion that took Frank back to the old days in The Red Lion, as he turned the key in the lock of his small apartment, turned to the street to shake the rainwater from his raincoat and hat and turned again to attach them to the small hooks in the porchway.

As he walked through the doorway to the lounge, the simple thought occurred to him, for the first time since Percy's narrative years ago, that if Fox considered the wearing or the removal of hats in church, or anywhere else, to be a frivolous thing, then it seemed to follow that the insistence that hats be removed was as silly as the insistence that they should remain *in situ*. After all, Fox himself had said that Quakerism was not all about hats; his religion was not all about the etiquette of hats. Ergo, insistence in such matters was absurd, either way: what was sauce for the goose was sauce for the gander, or, in this case, the Fox. Frank smiled as he walked to the kitchen to make himself a cup of tea. Of course, hats, whether worn or removed, might well be of symbolic significance; but then Fox himself had not considered imprisonment to be at all a suitable price to pay for it; it was, for him and any other reasonable being, a sacrifice not worth making if it entailed loss of freedom in a miserable cell and a forced diet of bread and water. How right he had been! Frank lamented the fact that hats were not now so fashionable as they had been in his youth; indeed, in his youth few men would have felt properly dressed without a hat or something that might pass for one. Nowadays, the majority of men, and indeed women, were hatless. In any case, Frank himself had had his fair share of Scripture; as a small boy, and even somewhat older, he had been obliged to attend Sunday School, and, as far as he could recall, Christ himself had made no reference to hats; in fact, he satisfied himself that one would be hard put to find any reference to hats at all in the New Testament.

Henry might throw in his 'It's a question of priorities', but what kind of Scriptural priority could one possibly attach to hats? Frank thought of poor Henry when he and Percy had gone to visit him in a small side-ward in hospital; Henry was heavily sedated and was not expected to last the night; they had been told to be quiet and to remember that there could be no more than two visitors a time at his bedside; this last rule seemed to lack all priority, because Percy and Frank were his only visitors – there was no one else in his life, and even that was now ebbing away without his even knowing it. But the rule about being quiet made some sense; after all, a hospital was not a place to paint the town red. Frank wore a hat; Percy a cap; and they both took them off when they entered the room – as a sign of respect, or of pending loss, or who knows what? It would have made no material difference had they kept them on, and, in either case, it would not have been an offence demanding a prison sentence.

Poor Henry had worn a hat, and he had often kept it on in The Red Lion, while the smoke curled up from his pipe underneath it. (Until, that is, smoking was banned not only in all public places on pain of due process of law, but in all motorised vehicles, whether or not the owner of the vehicle in question happened to own it, so that what had once been a popular joke, that one day you would not be allowed to smoke in your own house or garden, was fast becoming a plausible prospect and was therefore no longer amusing.) But at least Henry's hat did not cover his face, and you knew it was Henry, not someone else masquerading as Henry. These days a woman might cover her face, and you would not know whether she smiled or frowned or indeed whether it was a woman at all. Apparently it was important to cover her face, though no one could give a convincing reason why, and despite the fact that there was no Scriptural justification for doing so, it would be interesting to know what such a justification could possibly look like. But perhaps a time could come when justification was not sought, when the very notion of justification had been buried and forgotten and that any attempt to resurrect it was punishable. By darker analogy, there must have been a time when brown shirts and black shirts and Swastika armbands had become commonplace in Nazi Germany – so commonplace that they were unquestioned; so commonplace that the distinction between unquestioned and unquestionable had quite evaporated.

Frank did not bother to draw any hard and fast conclusion from these cerebral meanderings, if indeed there were one to draw. He sensed that there were weightier matters, ones which may require a stronger beverage than tea to contemplate. And he was drawn back to the idea that *the power of the Lord went over the nation.* Perhaps it was this that led to the absurdities of trivia, and then these that led to imprisonment and the cruelties suffered therein, many of them described by Percy on the authority of Fox himself, and to other inhumanities too despicable to relate.

5
Words, Words, Words

Of these three men, Percy had been the wordsmith, being far more widely read than his job demanded. He had always gone overboard in everything he did. It was not enough to know his subject; it was necessary to go between and behind the lines. He regarded his historical investigations as a journey – long, winding and unreliable – and because you could never know who was really telling the truth, you were stuck with words; words were the only source of certainty, for words meant what they meant, and that was that; everything else had to be taken on trust, if taken at all.

Unsurprisingly, therefore, one of Percy's catchphrases was, 'It's a question of definition.' Percy's insistence on definition might often have seemed gratuitous, hair-splitting and indeed bloody-minded. But in poor Percy's defence, one might with some justice be moved to reflect that the quest for definition can hardly be overdone since most people seldom seem to know what they mean by what they say on rather abstract matters, and therefore can rarely say what they mean, if they mean anything at all – which is why, perhaps, people are so bad at thinking, words being the building blocks of ideas. And on those rare occasions when they know what they mean by what they say, they signally fail to convey what they mean to the rest of us. Percy had never gone in for crosswords despite his love of words, simply because he was afraid of becoming addicted to them, as many of his colleagues had been, and many of his counterparts in teacher staffrooms round the world; crosswords were all very well, but there were more pressing demands on his time and on his thinking.

This time, when Percy announced 'It's a question of definition', one evening in The Red Lion, he was thinking in particular about the words that were frequently in the mouths of George Fox & co., in statements like 'The Lord's power went over the nation'. After all, the reference to power might easily inspire the reflection that power, however benevolent in concept and in its beginnings, might well take a turn for the worse; after all, Lord Acton had long ago pointed out, for the instruction of mankind, that all power tends to corrupt and absolute power corrupts absolutely – sadly a piece of wisdom that invariably falls on deaf ears, to the unspeakable cost of the innocent and the good; certain terrible facts about human nature seemed to be incontrovertible, subject to the kind of endorsement that The Bard himself gives to true love: *If this be error, and upon me proved, I never writ, nor no man ever loved.* And as for *Lord*, many have been so named and proved false, like promises in the wind. Lords, like gods, may take many forms, and obedience to them may well become a form of subservience; it was so important to give one's allegiance, if one gave it to anyone at all, to the *right* lord, and who or what the right lord is was not a matter that seemed to command universal consent; hence the importance of definition, a matter that few seemed to be aware of. A lord is a leader, and Percy recalled that the German word for leader is *Führer,* and the world had had quite enough of the *Führerprinzip!*

Percy knew that a word is more than a mere configuration of letters. Words needed to be spelt correctly and pronounced correctly and they had meaning; and correctness in their use Percy found most reassuring. In a world where much was changing, words, rather like human nature, changed little if at all. He was doubtful whether an unchanging human nature was desirable, in view of its more serious shortcomings; but the relatively unchanging world of words was reassuring; after all, it was not as if their meaning changed according to the day of the week or the time of day. He seemed to like nothing better than the kind of journey that words offered him; he would often speak about his travels through a dictionary; starting with the need to find one word in particular, he would find himself branching off to look at others, stopping here and there as though on a punctuated journey, just as one might journey from London to Rome, stopping off at Paris and Brussels *en route*.

He explained as much to Frank and Henry when they were debating one evening whether travel broadens the mind. Percy thought that travel seldom broadens anything except the waistline, an excuse for filling one's stomach with foreign delights and regretting it afterwards. They thought Percy's fascination with words rather eccentric; they listened good-naturedly and said nothing, as they usually did whenever Percy piped up. But there was rather more to it than a harmless eccentricity. Percy, though not steeped in the rigours of academia, did however have a reasonable perception of the importance of words in relation to action. History and a little reflection had taught him that words make sentences and that sentences express ideas, and that ideas are the springs of action. People acted, or decided not to act, in response to ideas; and since words were the elements of ideas, it was essential to get them right. Beliefs embodied ideas, and beliefs could either make us or break us, and invariably they were better at breaking than making.

Percy himself had a belief. He believed that history should be taught to invite life-lessons. It was not a fashionable view; it was best to keep such beliefs under wraps when the school inspectors were abroad; when inspectors entered the classroom, it was eyes down for a bunch of names and dates; but when inspectors were left out of the equation, Percy wanted to teach history differently; he believed that those who forget their past are in danger of repeating its mistakes, which was not an original conception of how history should be taught but was, in practice, a principle rarely satisfactorily and courageously applied. The usual way of teaching the subject was not for him; it was like teaching pure mathematics as though applied mathematics never existed, and he was intensely interested in application. And since children were the future, they needed to be protected from the follies of the past, at least insofar as protection was at all feasible, and even this was a subject for debate – but one had to do one's best. Yes, it might fairly be said that Percy regarded himself as a man on a mission. (A belief that would not bode well for his own future, as we shall see.) And there was an abundance of past follies to appeal to in the hope that they would never be repeated again in the lifetime of the youngsters he taught: the destruction of the great libraries of Constantinople; the public burning of books in Nazi Germany, all in the name of the Führer; the burning of the written word amongst the Taliban and Islamic fanatics, all in the name of their Lord – and all this the application of power, power in the hands of those who were bound to abuse it, since their beliefs, the basic elements of which were words, demanded abuse, since it is hard to imagine brainwashing in the absence of words.

'It's a question of definition,' said Percy.

'Look out! He's gonna hold forth!' said Henry, good-naturedly.

'Let's get a round in first,' Frank put in.

'Well, trouble depends on words,' said Percy, when the rounds were in. 'That George Fox and his chums said "Thee" and "Thou" and that got them into trouble, and the word "Quaker" was meant to denigrate these people – tit for tat, trouble for trouble, y'see?'

'You had to *tremble* at the name of the Lord,' said Frank.

'Right,' said Henry.

'And in those days,' Percy went on, 'the word "witch" could be the end of you!'

'Like the word "racist" today,' said Frank, taking a quick look round the pub, which was by now filling up quite nicely.

'Exactly,' said Percy, lowering his voice and nodding deeply, as though he had at last discovered a kindred spirit after years of hopeless searching.

'Yeah, but we've moved on a lot since then. We don't burn racists, thank goodness!' said Henry, perhaps not fully realising how much he really had to thank *goodness*.

'Not yet!' said Frank, with a broad grin. 'Not yet.'

Yes, they all agreed that words could make you or break you in one way or another. The Quakers were ridiculed by their critics for their wordless meetings – 'What edification is there here where there are no words?' And, says George Fox, these critics claimed never to have seen the like in their lives before. To whom Fox retorts that despite the vast number of words spoken to them by their priests in own churches, there is shockingly little edification, but only a means of persuasion to part with their money. At least Fox understood, like the Native Americans of the Great Plains, that many words, like rich garments, do not maketh a good man and that silence, like gold, can be enriching. And so, the Quakers in their meetings would sit in silence, awaiting the Power of their Lord to invest Friends with His spirit so that, the job having been done, words might flow, yet never to excess, almost as though these Friends were so shocked by the excesses of human vice that, like the old man who lived alone on a hill, they found themselves unable to do anything but utter inarticulate sounds. The springs of silence may be many and varied, so that silence itself might be welcome or unwelcome, as the springs demand. Silence might, after all, be a boon, like an army disarmed.

'Not much chance of that here,' mumbled Henry, as the pub filled up. It was Friday night, and gradually the hum of voices, the tinkling of glasses and the scraping of chairs became more noticeable.

He was right. Occasionally, Frank, Henry, and yes, even Percy, sat in silence, so that their presence resembled a Quaker meeting with periods of wordlessness punctuated by the occasional observation. But theirs were not the only voices that rose above the general hubbub on those occasions when they strained to hear each other speak. For, like most northern pubs, The Red Lion had its fair share of 'characters', two of whom are worthy of mention, since one relied on words for her very identity, and the other, well, he relied on them not at all.

She was known to our three friends as The Yellow Rose of Texas, though that comely flower, had it ever bloomed in her at all, had wilted long ago, a fact to which the loose skin which formed a patchwork of folds on her face and neck, and the bulging veins that criss-crossed the backs of her hands spoke volumes in testimony; her still abundant hair, now greyish-white, might yet appear somewhat yellow when she stood near enough to the bar to be illuminated by the little lights that overhung it; but the illusion of youth simply could not be sustained. She must have been in her very late sixties at least, probably older; her precise age was never confirmed, though she would announce her birthday quite openly, knowing full well that the announcement would produce a few free drinks at the bar; it was widely rumoured that, on her own authority, she had been sixty for years, and people with sufficient interest were obliged to settle for that, for on this subject at least she was anything but loose-tongued. On any other subject she was a veritable torrent of words, especially when it came to matters of health.

'We should call her "Calamity Jane",' Frank had suggested. 'Her life's full of it.' But 'The Yellow Rose of Texas' had stuck firmly and could not be changed except by statute. After a few beers, she was wont to visit people at their tables and relate to them, in particular to those she knew best and who had proved to possess the patience of Job, the latest maladies to have assailed her: sore joints, a stiff back, bruises and abrasions on knees and elbows, loose teeth, blistered feet, and other, more private, inconveniences, to which she would merely allude with a nod or a wink and perhaps the phrase 'women's things'. She wore, almost with the regularity of a uniform, loose-fitting slacks and an old anorak, and she was known to lift up the legs of the former and open up the latter to reveal, if appropriate, the very malady to which she referred, expecting an outpouring of sundry sympathetic nods and utterances in response. Having observed her stiff knee once, one knew what to expect when the subject came up again and lived in the abiding hope that the source of that particular malady would not be revealed a second time until one had quite recovered from the unwelcome sight – which was invariably never.

That lady with her vast store of medical misfortunes was not, however, actively avoided by those who came to know her; for she was also known to be kind, and known to give a sympathetic hearing, if not a helpful hand, to others if it was at all possible for her to do so. She was known to all as 'harmless', which meant that her intrusions at table, her long-winded explanations of trivia accompanied by her physical demonstrations of maladies-at-source should all be tolerated as a reward for her own virtues and even, perhaps, as giving her an incentive to go living at all in a world which would otherwise ignore and abandon her and thus consign her to oblivion. Despite her limited vocabulary, words were her link to people and to life.

And if The Yellow Rose of Texas was indisposed and temporarily unavailable, there was always Wild Bill Hickok, as he was known to our three, to perform the kind offices of unintentional entertainment. Unintentional, because Wild Bill, who was somewhere in his early to mid-seventies, seemed to take himself quite seriously, even if no one else could possibly do so. True, he appeared to be wild enough: his black cowboy hat sat atop a grey, stubbly face so tightly drawn and hollow-cheeked, it was only one degree from skeletal; his eyes were sunken, and his black waistcoat hugged his poor frame, for he looked dreadfully thin, indeed emaciated; while his black drainpipe trousers, held up with a black belt and a large silver buckle, hugged his matchstick legs; one might be forgiven for thinking that his clothes were intended to hold this poor specimen precariously and temporarily together before Nature itself, out of an uncomfortable mixture of sheer pity and intolerable embarrassment, offered a gentle *coup de grace.* Despite this, he seemed to go on forever … and forever.

Wild Bill, however, seemed to rely mainly on appearance and less on words for any credibility that he thought he might muster. It is, nevertheless, in the nature of words that they get around, and that, like water, they find their way into every nook and cranny. And so, Wild Bill had let it be known that during his astonishing lifetime he had been variously employed as street-fighter, secret agent, mercenary soldier and member of the very elite SAS. Interestingly, Custer's Chief of Scouts had been left out of his list of achievements – possibly because even Wild Bill had some sense of historical veracity and had decided to omit it for the sake of preserving his credibility amongst those who might possibly know better. Our three friends had nevertheless decided to christen him with the name of that notorious gunfighter who, on some authorities, had been favoured by Calamity Jane who, for her troubles, became a victim of unrequited love.

Apparently satisfied in the belief that word had amply got around, Wild Bill would simply walk round the The Red Lion, occasionally doffing his cap to this or that table, as though making his final rounds to a doting audience, namely the pub's patrons, before finally shaking off his mortal coil, though, as already hinted, it was a coil that would require a very great deal of shaking off despite the fragility of his frame and what seemed to be the incontrovertible evidence of his imminent physical disintegration and final demise.

It might fairly be said, therefore, that Wild Bill was never stuck for words, if only because he had abandoned them long ago in favour of a doff here and a doff there. Words had already set the scene; they had done their job; it now only remained for Wild Bill to take to the stage, which he certainly did, and with a relish that can only be admired and rarely encountered save in the greatest of hearts. He was a comic caricature of an imagined heroic figure, a Walter Mitty of The Red Lion, but, even in that regard, not entirely unlike those who made gentle fun of him but were not half as funny, not half as proud, not half as endearing, and, what is more, not half as alive.

6
Ascent and Descent

Words could make you or break you. They were the vehicles of beliefs, the soil in which beliefs were planted as seeds, and also the stones in which they were set. As for the latter, even the most cursory forage into history would confirm it, for who amongst the Nazis would venture to omit a *Sieg Heil!* whenever appropriate? Words might separate us from the animal kingdom, but they might also jettison us back into it, and even down to levels way lower than animals themselves could possibly endorse. It was tacitly agreed amongst the three friends that words were therefore to be treated with caution. That much, at least, was settled.

Frank and Henry also agreed, or, rather, would certainly have agreed had the matter ever been squarely put to them, that whatever goes up, must come down, and that going up and coming down might either proceed by almost imperceptible degrees or in fits and starts or in leaps and bounds. They probably would not have allowed that what goes up might go up so far that coming down again could never be an option; even less would they have agreed that what is 'up' and what is 'down' is sometimes incapable of definition, or that, in plain terms, which direction is up and which is down cannot always be determined. But they would have been fairly satisfied that what goes up can be expected to come down again, neatly in accordance with Newton's Laws of Motion and in conformity with day-to-day experience.

Percy, however, and as we shall see in the fullness of time, was not altogether comfortable about this commonplace approach to physics. But he certainly agreed about an observed fact: that very big things might have relatively small beginnings. They need only hark back, for example, to how The Red Lion looked in the heydays of Wild Bill and The Yellow Rose of Texas, for it had not simply been gestures and words that had sustained these two colourful personages; no, not at all; in fact, it entailed something of a feat of imagination to have pictured either of them without a smouldering cigarette that seemed to accompany each of them everywhere; they remembered how Wild Bill would doff his hat with one hand while clutching his cigarette in the other, and how The Yellow Rose of Texas would balance hers precariously on the edge of a beer mat while she fumbled with her trouser-leg to reveal the latest condition of her knee (how she failed to notice the ashtray placed on the table in front of her remained a mystery to all and sundry – but no doubt she was too engrossed in the provision of updates).

First, there was only *talk* about smokeless pubs – which no one took very seriously, for what was a pint without a cigarette? It would be risking the very identity of a pint to deprive the ambience of smoke-rings. No, the idea was preposterous (a word no one in The Red Lion would have used, if only because they would have been unable to pronounce it) and therefore could never possibly catch on. When the idea was first mooted, Henry, pipe in hand, was quick to dismiss it and actually waxed lyrical in the process, pointing out to Frank and Percy how important a pipe of tobacco had been to Johann Sebastian Bach, a composer that was very high on Percy's own list of indisputable geniuses, and quoting lines that were attributed to him: *So, o'er my pipe in contemplation of such matters, I can constantly indulge in fruitful meditation. Thus, puffing contentedly, I smoke my pipe and worship God.* Percy wondered whether Bach's God and the God of George Fox were one and the same, but he kept the thought to himself. No, said Henry, the idea of smokeless pubs just wouldn't catch on – not in his lifetime anyway, and he struck a match as if to dismiss the idea with the finality of a three-line whip.

But it did more than simply catch on, and in Henry's lifetime to boot. It became a question of *law*, and when things become questions of law they have come a very long way, rather like throwing a paper plane and watching it soar above a major airport *en route* for a transatlantic destination. That kind of transition beggars belief, and when things beggar belief, it's hard to find words to fit the occasion. There were no words for it. The effect on Wild Bill and The Yellow Rose of Texas was quite devastating, and their subsequent performances were somewhat subdued; like showmen who have been suddenly deprived of one of their props, they had to make do with whatever they had left. In fact, The Red Lion itself had somehow to adjust to toeing the line and becoming a lawful beast; the lion might roar, but it was obliged to acquiesce. The whole pub seemed to fall silent and began to resemble more a Quaker meeting-place than a sociable venue. However, whatever is enshrined in law, in a plethora of unpronounceable words and intricate phraseology, must be obeyed lest discovery of trespass lead to punishment, and punishment to closure – perish the thought! Everyone, the noble Lion included, must be brought to heel. The Law entails Power, for without power law is pointless, and power instils fear. (Why, the weak are even capable of attributing power to things that do not intrinsically possess it: it has been observed more than once by the wise men of old that the step between merely imagining something powerful and its actually being so is a very short one. The propensity towards fear is therefore incalculable.) But little did the three friends know that there was much, oh, much worse to come!

But something else was happening by degrees, too. Or so Frank and Henry felt, though they were careful to keep their fears from Percy, simply because their fears concerned Percy himself, and it was a most delicate and personal matter. One night, when Percy had gone to the bar to pay for the next round, Henry and Frank gave each other knowing looks accompanied by a slow shaking of heads. Percy had had some sort of bee in his bonnet for some time now and had returned to the subject that very night. He had simply said, out of the blue, *'Yesterday, the day before yesterday, and all our yesterdays, are one – and today is* tomorrow's *yesterday.'* He mumbled it vacantly, as though it were a kind of mantra he had learned off by heart. Frank and Henry stared as Percy came out of his trance and offered what was meant to pass for an explanation, but which turned out to be something that began to worry his two friends. 'Well, I mean, it's as though the Jewish holocaust were yesterday, and the Armenian holocaust was the day before yesterday – but, in point of fact, that's as far back as I can go with these horrors!' Frank pointed out that these horrors happened a long time ago. 'But that's just my point, you see' – Percy became animated – 'They *didn't*! I don't *feel* it that way, I can't *see* it that way – and the terrible thing is, it's all going to happen again *tomorrow*! It's all on the cards – everything! – *again*! – believe you me!' He seemed to settle back after this outburst. It was as though the phoenix, which is said to rise from the ashes, had at last ruffled its feathers in an effort to do so, before falling back into its original posture, the effort having perhaps proved excessively demanding. After a brief pause, 'Oh well!' was all Henry could say, which was to say nothing at all. Frank simply nodded, not knowing what to say; after all, what could one possibly say? The best thing was to let the matter drop gently, to say nothing; it was time to humour Percy, and to jog him back into reality by sending him to the bar on the pretext that it was his round.

After Percy's first animated approach on this theme, he seemed to become progressively more subdued, more withdrawn, like someone who had predicted a storm and had hurried indoors to escape its onslaught. He was not himself. Was this a descent into the dark avenues of depression? Or was it the onset of senility? Were they beginning to see a new Percy, before Percy, as they had known him, disappeared altogether, like an upturned vessel on the verge of sinking from sight to the bottomless depths of the pitch-black ocean bed? Perish the thought! Perhaps, after all, it was only a temporary aberration, a mere flight of eccentric fancy – in which case, Percy, the old Percy, would be restored as good as new. This latter was a reasonable expectation; he had spent his whole life teaching history; he was steeped in it; now, in retirement, it would be natural for him to entertain some strange ideas, for plain amusement, and nothing else. Henry and Frank would wait and see, and hope for the best.

Meanwhile, the mantra kept running through Frank's head: *Yesterday, the day before yesterday, and all our yesterdays, are one – and today is tomorrow's yesterday.* He kept reminding himself of the obvious, that what was past was past, that what was a long time ago was indeed a long time ago, that tomorrow was another, and hopefully, much better day, that our tomorrows must, at least to some degree, incorporate the lessons learned from the past, that civilisation is not static, let alone backward-looking, but dynamic; battles had already been fought, and, surely, they had been worth fighting. But he also remembered Percy staring into his glass as though spellbound by something peculiar and irremovable at the bottom of it. 'It's in the past!' Henry had said. 'Not for me!' Percy had replied. 'Not for me!' Percy's reluctance to relegate the horrors of history to the past, where, after all, they rightly belong, was an abiding mystery to his two friends and simply pointed to Percy's descent into something dark and unstoppable. After all, so much for all our yesterdays, but what about *today*? But as Percy saw it, today is simply tomorrow's yesterday.

There was, however, another possibility, though it was admittedly a very long shot. Perhaps Percy really did have something to say. His sensing of continuity with the past was perhaps a form of heightened moral sensitivity, and to such an extent that it had become a kind of emotional mortgage that could never really be paid off. After all, all the ingredients were present: Percy was a good man, and as a serious student of history, of history that was more than the mere ability to recall dates and names, he would be in a better position than most good men to understand, and therefore revile, the horrors of the past. What he was expressing might just be the outpouring of all his repugnance, and of all his fears for the future. He was, in short, a good man who knew too much for his own good. Frodo, the good Hobbit, was pierced by a sword of a Dark Rider and he never wholly recovered from the wound, it being a constant reminder of his trials and tribulations. Might it not be something like that with Percy?

If this apparently more positive interpretation of Percy's condition was at all credible, then perhaps he was a man, not in descent, but in the ascendant; perhaps, as a man with something important to say, he was going places and on the up. Henry laughed out loud at his own thoughts when he shared them with Frank, who was equally amused. They both knew that such conjectures, even if they made sense, were quite over the top. After all, Percy was about to turn seventy, reaching his biblical allotment of three score and ten; and it was more likely that he was, poor fellow, a man in the descendent. In any case, and not forgetting that what goes up must come down, Percy had better be careful what he came out with next, for a disposition to say something extremely incisive may well land him in trouble in these changing times. After all, if smokeless pubs were possible, who knows what might be next? Frank and Henry enjoyed the joke, and quickly returned to the thought that poor Percy was in all probability losing his grip on reality. It was their job, as his best of friends, to try to ensure than the transition was as painless as possible while all the time hoping for a return to the normal and the familiar. This talk of all our yesterdays being one smacked of a kind of merger of long- and short-term memory, a breakdown of the distinction between the there-and-then and the here-and-now – a sure sign of mental decline if ever there was one. This was the worrying thing.

But it was not so simple, either.

Percy was very well aware of the perceived 'merger' of past and present and future; of course he was, for it was precisely this that he *explicitly* expounded. A man who is aware of his impending insanity is hardly insane. A defendant may plead guilty-but-insane, but then it is not he *himself* who does the pleading, but the Counsel for Defence on his behalf. Percy's stuff about a temporal merger of past, present and future was presented in the form of some kind of theory, however eccentric it may sound, however contrary to common sense. It is a question of logical priority: first, a theory must make sense; if it does not make sense, there is little more to be said; if it does make sense, it is possible to go on to determine whether it is true or false. Perhaps, after all, what Percy said made sense; but, even so, it might still turn out false – but then the problem would be to find a way of deciding this. Neither Henry nor Frank felt able even to decide whether what Percy was going on about made sense at all; they were therefore precluded from determining whether it was true or false. What was certain was that Percy himself was fully aware of what he was saying, or trying to say; and this did not seem to count as evidence in favour of insanity, impending or otherwise. No, the whole thing was anything but simple.

And things did not stop there, either.

Percy was ready to expound further, to elaborate and introduce notions that seemed ever more fantastic. 'Passage through time isn't linear at all,' he announced. Frank and Henry looked at each other; they had by now formed an unwritten and unspoken pact: to listen, wait and hope for the best. 'No,' Percy went on, 'it's just a circular, spiralling continuum. Y'see?' Of course, they did not see, and they wondered whether Percy saw, either. But 'patience' was the watchword. It now sounded as though Percy was expounding some kind of astrophysics, and whether or not it made any sense at all, either as physics or as anything else, was way beyond their competence to say; the further worry, of course, is that it was probably beyond Percy's competence, too.

That night, Henry dreamed a dream as crazy as Percy's pronouncements. He saw Percy whirling skyward and out into the stratosphere, becoming a whirling circling mass of light, dodging in and out of the stars, circling ever faster until he became a circle of intense brightness, at which point Henry woke up with the sun in his eyes, having forgotten to close the curtains the previous night.

Henry had not slept well, not for a number of weeks now, to which he attributed his feelings of sluggishness, his constant under-the-weather indisposition. There was nothing in particular to point to, no pain as such; just a general loss of appetite, and even the beer in The Red Lion had somehow lost its savour, as though it had been watered down – he had joked about it one evening to Malcolm the proprietor, who had rounded on him for it. 'No, no, it must be me – one of those things,' Henry had replied apologetically, and then all was well again, except that the beer continued to be unsatisfying, and to such an extent that Henry cared little whether he drank it or not. What was happening? he wondered. Perhaps life itself was losing its savour. 'Bah! Such thoughts. Come on now!' And, like everyone else, Henry tried hard to pick himself up from the floor of despair and get on with things – what else was there to do? What else, indeed?

And when he thought of Percy, he did not know whether to feel pleased with himself by comparison or more depressed at the thought that he himself might start to speak just as eccentrically. He hated the thought of losing Percy, the Percy he had long known. And what about Frank? Suppose, for example, Frank began to think that one day the world would be ruled by the crow family? Suppose he went about arguing that the crows and the rooks and the ravens, and even the magpies, would do a far better job of ruling the world than human beings had done? Suppose he argued that the crows were watching from their rooftops and chimneys just waiting for an opportunity to take control, and that the nattering between them, all that kaawing and croaking, was simply the planning stage of the takeover, the preparatory decision-making of the future kings of the earth, and that human beings would be pecked out of existence, their corpses left to rot and stiffen and whiten, just as the carcasses of birds are left on our roads and fields? Suppose old Frank started to talk like that? What would become of him? And what would become of Henry? But, for the moment, the question mark hung over Percy, and what to make of it all.

It did not, perhaps could not possibly, occur to either Frank or Henry, that what Percy was trying to say had nothing at all to do with physics, astro or otherwise, or any kind of science at all, unless, that is, the *human* or *social* sciences were included. Had he been able to stand apart from it all, he might have decided to retract it all, to delete it, realising that he was merely endeavouring to find a language of expression to say what many a good man had seen through a glass somewhat darkly and on that account failed to express satisfactorily. By the same token, perhaps George Fox would have surrendered his 'Lord' and his 'Thee' and his 'Thou', and even his refusal to swear oaths, had he managed to find an alternative lexis, an alternative mode of expression; but we are all the victims of our own time and the language we speak is not of our own making; we are stuck with what we find, as we are stuck with the language in which beliefs are embedded, and therefore stuck, for good or ill, with the beliefs that emerge from words like flowers and weeds from the soil in which they grow.

Frank and Henry might have understood, had they been of a particular turn of mind, a mind that would have stood in relation to Percy's as a marriage of minds, that Percy was not expressing the possible findings of science, but a refusal to let things go as though they never happened at all, yes, a refusal to bury the follies of the past under a heap of mediocrity, a refusal to comprehend that the horrors of the past were as real in the present as ever they had been in the past.

But in all this, he was also refusing to let sleeping dogs lie, which would account for the vague and unarticulated unease with which Henry and Frank viewed what they saw as Percy's probable mental decline, namely that the poor fellow might say too much out loud and end up creating more trouble for himself than he could possibly handle, and more trouble than he deserved. Indeed, had they known it, or had they put the matter squarely to Percy himself, who did know it, he might end up like George Fox himself who, for all his trouble to follow Christ, spent a large part of his life in and out of jail on charges for the most part trumped up, or perverse according to Scripture.

7

And Then There Were Two

In strict accordance with the ironies of life, which appear to strike with a regularity attributable to Swiss clockwork, Percy's perceived descent was preceded by Henry's.

As he lay in a hospital bed, a return home having been ruled out, all he could hope for was palliative care for a stomach cancer which, he was told, was rare and aggressive. He had time enough, however, to ruminate, and first among his ruminations was the thought that if Percy was losing it, it might have been better if he himself had lost it and been incapable now of all ruminations; there were times and circumstances in which the ability to think might be intolerable, and this was one of them. As for his own decline, he could not with any precision say when it had started. All he knew is that it must have started some time, though he had not been feeling himself for a long time now. How things could happen like this was bewildering, how life could start and end, how descent must follow ascent, how what goes up must come down – this was incomprehensible; life was full of beginnings and endings; beginnings were as mysterious as endings: he had often paused to wonder how fruit flies, for example, could simply come into being without so much as a by-your-leave; one day there was a bunch of bananas in a fruit bowl, the next these accursed little beasts were flying hither and thither from God knows where; and then there were maggots – how on earth did they spring into being, like magic, from nowhere? He remembered from his schooldays the Bard's observation that nothing comes from nothing. But King Lear's cutting remark said nothing about the something from which other things spring. Life seemed like a faceless clock, with the hands in continual motion, pointing to nothing that could resemble an explanation; and this reminded him of Percy again. Even so, a study of microbiology would most likely have left Henry asking the very same questions; for these questions were not the sort that could ever be answered by science, any more than Percy's stuff about the space-time continuum of inhumanities could earn him the respect of astrophysicists. Henry could make neither head nor tail of human existence, just as Percy was left speechless by man's inhumanity to man. Why do things have to begin? And, perhaps more importantly, why do they have to end? And as for what is in the middle, well, that often passes unnoticed, until one is obliged to notice because the end is knocking hard on one's door. As for the knocking on the door, Henry was most disinclined to notice it; to help him ignore it, Percy and Frank, in the first few days of their friend's hospitalisation, smuggled a small packet of his favourite pipe tobacco into the ward for Henry to smoke surreptitiously somewhere outside whenever he might have a chance; Henry quickly hid it amongst the items in his little bedside locker, where it was found after his demise – unopened.

Henry's bedridden reflections turned every which way; when they were not about beginnings and ends, on ascent and descent, they focused on his own private life. His thoughts frequently turned on his marriage, and Sylvia, his late wife. He managed to smile at the phrase 'late wife'; whatever she was, she was never ever *late*! On the contrary, she was as punctual and punctilious as a sergeant major on parade; had it not been for her, Henry would have been late for work every day of his working life – on the assumption, of course, that he would have survived in a job at all, and not been successively dismissed from one job after another. She was the same about the house, and eventually it rubbed off on Henry himself who, since her passing, had adopted the habit of picking up the least crumb from the carpet at the expense of his lumbago, of frequently puffing up the cushions, which hardly ever needed puffing up, and of never leaving dishes unwashed until the following morning – it was as though, in her absence, he had taken on some of her memorable characteristics as a means of keeping her somehow alive. Almost each time he picked up a crumb, the irresistible thought bore down on him, *Well, she wouldn't want it any other way.* Even now, therefore, although he lived quite alone, the place was spick and span, as though ready lest Sylvia – oh blessed miracle! – should walk through the door, as she used to do after the weekly shop in the high street.

It had been what most people would consider a very successful and cosy marriage, amply evidenced, after all, by the fact that not a day passed when Henry did not speak to his wife despite the fact that she was now *in absentia aeterna.* The questions *What would she say? What would she do?* were frequently on his lips or else were unspoken mental inquisitions. Even before her passing, the world was in a state of rapid flux, and what she would say about everything now, given how the world was turning out, did not bear thinking about. 'Just as well you're not here, Sylvia,' he would sometimes find himself muttering. But, of course, it was not just as well at all – but there was nothing at all he or anyone else could do to bring her back.

As far as their more intimate relationship was concerned, Henry had been faithful to a fault – not that he had had many opportunities to be otherwise. His thoughts would sometimes wander in and out of imagined opportunities and alternative adventures, for his own relationship had long ceased to be an adventure at all. 'Mind you, when I come to think of it …' but he could only think of those three, possibly four, occasions when he might have allowed himself to kiss someone else as though he meant it, and that's really as far as he could go in this train of thought. No, it had to be admitted that he had been faithful to a fault – the fault being that though he had been unquestionably and unfailingly faithful to Sylvia, he had perhaps neglected to be faithful to himself. Now, on his own and in his hospital bed with little prospect of ever leaving it, his life appeared to have been quite sacrificial. But it was invidious to pursue this line of thought – and quite pointless. No, if it had been a sacrifice, it had been one well worth making; he began to feel most apologetic, 'Sorry, Sylvia, my dear!' he imagined telling her, as though she were standing at the foot of the bed. No, he had taken a most solemn oath, a promise, and such things cannot be broken. But here he recalled Percy's ramblings one evening in The Red Lion; something about that fellow George Fox again, and his refusal to swear oaths, which landed him in prison on more than one occasion and almost cost him his life – refusing to take the Oath of Allegiance to the King, or something like that, and allowing Quaker marriages unsolemnised by oaths. Old George, as Henry had called him in one unsuccessful attempt after another to pull poor Percy's leg, thought that since Jesus Christ had ruled against the swearing of oaths in the Sermon on the Mount ('But I say unto you, swear not at all'), no Christian could be a Christian worthy of the name unless he practised what Christ had commanded. So, oaths were out – though Henry, despite asking Percy to elucidate and then going through the awful experience of having to listen to Percy's prolonged and droning elucidations, was none the wiser afterwards than when he started; on the contrary, Henry felt fully and truly immersed in extremely murky waters; he had been forced, for the sake of his own sanity, to let the matter rest. Anyway, whatever the Gospels were according to Old George, Henry had taken an oath, made a promise, and he had spent forty years of married life upholding it, never departing from it, never infringing it – despite those occasions when, being human and therefore subject to and suffering from all the design faults that being human implied, none of them, incidentally, of his own making, his attentions, like stray sheep on the lookout for pastures greener, were apt to momentarily wander – yes, despite those rare, perhaps not quite so rare, occasions when his imaginings, if translated into action, would have implied a serious breach of solemn promise. Yes, loyalty complete and absolute, or almost complete and absolute – at least in deed, and, for the most part, in thought. And that, thought he, was the *Power of Love.* Had Henry written the phrase, he would almost certainly have employed capitals. Henry could see little problem with oaths that sprang from love; as for Old George, since he had believed in a punishing God, his convictions on other matters were hardly to be trusted. Good people, thought Henry, do a splendid job punishing themselves, and a God of Love, which is what any God worthy of the name must be, should be busily employed pouring balm on the wounds that good people inflict on themselves. There were oaths and there were oaths; and to rule out oaths that were expressions of love seemed to Henry as absurd and regrettable as the outlawing of pork amongst the Muslims, or of beef amongst the Hindus; if one's faith were an amalgam of religions, one would be well on the way to a starvation diet; and a recourse to vegetarianism or veganism would risk fanatical representations in favour of Vegetable Rights! No, it had to be said that the design faults in human beings went pretty deep, with the possible and tragic corollary that they were incapable of repair.

Such was the ebb and flow of Henry's thoughts as he lay in that hospital bed surrounded by pretty nurses, unfettered as he now was by the promise he had kept all his life, but fettered still, why yes, of course, fettered now by old age and disease and the none-too-distant prospect of shaking off his mortal coil with an attendant loss of dignity. He smiled at himself; after all these years, his youth having flown long ago like some mythical bird in an ancient fairy story, and his lying now prostrate and dependent, with a future short and painful – yes, despite all this, he could still imagine a nurse or two entertaining a wish to get to know him intimately. He tended to fall immediately in love with every new nurse that entered the ward; the idea of love at first sight took on a broader and deeper significance for the first time in his life, and he fancied himself waltzing around the ward with every pretty face, each lucky nurse snuggling into his warm and confident embrace, quite forgetting that he was never in his life capable of taking a step, no, not even to save his life. He saw himself as a comic figure, and managed a chuckle. Try as he might, he could not imagine Sylvia looking down on him from high and wishing him all the best in his amorous fantasies; it was far, far too late for second chances – the whole idea was ridiculous, if not faintly embarrassing, if not slightly obscene. 'Too late. Too late.' These words were like barbed arrows. Chilling words. Sobering words. Words to bring you down from your heights. Words to cool the brain. Words to prepare you for eternity – if anything at all could prepare you for that! In any case, he hoped and prayed that Sylvia would forgive him for thoughts that were as unacceptable now as they had always been. He was only *human* after all, and there was a limit to what could be expected from humans. There would shortly come a time when Henry would be moved out of the general ward and when his ruminations, of whatever kind, would all but cease, and then cease altogether. For now, however, he was inclined to fall repeatedly in love with a mere idea, for mere ideas were now all he had.

And at this stage of his hospitalisation, there were moments and circumstances that served to lighten his mood, for Henry's sense of humour, which had always helped to keep him going through thick and thin, did not desert him now in his hour of direst need. Being in a general ward, which, due to the inadvisability of allowing geriatric patients to go home in circumstances where they could not receive round-the-clock attention, sought to accommodate them until alternative arrangements could be made, Henry found himself in the company of two very old gentlemen who, for all they knew, or cared, might have been guests in a five-star hotel; due to senility, they were blissfully unaware of their real surroundings, and to such an extent that poor Henry found himself a spectator in a theatre of the absurd. While he was still capable of doing so, Henry would laugh himself to sleep; the gods are therefore sometimes kind to those who wait on their threshold.

In the bed to Henry's left was an old fellow called Martin, who seemed to be in and out of reality like the cuckoo in a clock. One moment he would appear to be looking quite engaged in reading an article in a newspaper, and therefore mentally alert; the next he would be staring into space like a waxwork model, or else he would be attempting a mission impossible, by endeavouring to clamber out of bed and into his Zimmer frame, which stood close by, despite the fact that some of the tubes in his arms were attached to a machine immovably fixed to the wall behind his bed – the whole effort, therefore, was necessarily a case of one step forward and two steps back, with Martin falling flat on his back on top of the bed. Nor did he seem capable of learning from failed attempts; and each time a nurse had to be called by a patient not as far gone as Martin himself.

It was during the night, when the lights were out and everybody was expected to sleep, that Martin's antics became almost amusing. One of the doors of a room leading off the ward would not close in one go, but rather shut with a series of knocking noises whenever a medic opened it and passed through. Martin, in one of his half-in and half-out states, must have thought he was home and that someone was knocking the door. 'Come in!' he would shout, in the darkness. After a few moments the door would elicit a second shout, louder than before, Martin obviously becoming a little impatient, 'I said, come in!!' and then a third time, 'For God's sake, come in! What's the matter with you!!!' The only hope was that the night sedatives that he had been given would finally take effect, that he would get off to sleep and let everyone else off the hook.

But Martin's nightly excursions into fantasy were as nothing compared to those of the elderly and senile patient whose bed stood opposite Henry's, and whom Henry christened King Arthur. During the daylight hours, Arthur was quiet enough, but shortly after lights-out he would begin to hold court with a gathering of imaginary characters who, presumably, were thought to sit or stand round his bed. Arthur's intonation really did suggest that he might be discussing weighty matters of state, but all Henry could make out was an interminable string of incomprehensible sounds; Arthur's court lasted for as long as Arthur felt he had something to say, until, that is, he fell asleep and his courtiers had been dismissed; the whole episode lasted the space of two or three hours, sedatives clearly having had little effect on Arthur himself, and necessarily no effect at all on his doting courtiers; no wonder he was subdued in the daytime!

One day, a large armchair was placed next to Arthur's bed, perhaps in an attempt to minimise the development of bed sores, and Arthur was enthroned upon it, in a State Ceremony that many might have paid to see. Arthur was clearly content with his throne. Unfortunately, the armchair, being orthopaedic and state-of-the-art, could be adjusted electronically; Arthur began fiddling with the handheld control panel, perhaps believing it to be the TV remote control used at home. The result was near-catastrophic; Arthur pressed the button which regulated the forward and backward position of the back of the chair; the chair-back proceeded to buzz and whirr its way forward so that at any moment Arthur would be ejected forcibly onto the floor, his reign being prematurely cut short in favour of some undeserving usurper and power-grabber. The king was caught in time, his reign preserved, his kingdom saved. Needless to say, the handheld remote panel was kept well hidden thereafter.

Had his hospital stay been temporary and only routine, Henry would have held forth in The Red Lion about Martin and King Arthur. Frank and Percy would have seen the funny side of things, and they would all have laughed together. They would have teased him about his falling in love with all the nurses. But things also had a deeper, more reflective side: for while all the nurses, pretty or not, were kind and competent, they were not the faces Henry had grown up with; most of the medics spoke English with foreign accents and their faces were Asian or Mediterranean. They would all have agreed that such things should not matter, that they should not be items in anyone's consideration; yet, somehow it mattered – or perhaps it was simply nostalgia knocking on a familiar door and finding that the old occupants had moved away who-knows-where; such feelings would be natural, and without malice.

For there was no denying that the world, and that of the three friends in particular, had changed, and was still changing fast. Every day was a new chapter. If life were a book, it was getting increasingly difficult to read, harder to keep up, harder to predict. After all, look what was happening to Henry himself! Something very bad that neither Frank nor Percy could have predicted – no, not even Percy, for all his erudition.

During their hospital visits, Frank and Percy would chat with Henry with an increasing openness, due no doubt to the gravity of Henry's condition. Henry actually voiced the concerns that he and Frank had had about Percy's state of mind, when they had thought that Percy was in a vortex of descent. They all laughed about it. 'Nothing wrong with *you*, though, Percy! Funny, isn't it? That's how things go,' Henry said. But after Henry was moved off the general ward and into a room of his own, conversation became more difficult until it all but stopped. Frank and Percy simply sat watching him, and at first they tried to get through to him. At such times it is hard to know what to say; silence is unacceptable, yet they found themselves breaking the silence with silly things like, 'When you're better, Henry, we can all go on a trip together,' Frank muttered to his still and prostrate and almost lifeless friend. 'Yes, that's it,' Percy nodded. It was impossible to say whether Henry had heard this or not. It was well-meaning nonsense; but what mattered was that it sprang from love, just as an oath or a promise that cannot possibly be kept might spring from love; it was the *source* of nonsense that mattered – the origin, not the outcome.

Henry slipped away between visits, into what we should like to think of as an eternal rest. Whether he had seen a big white light in the process, or sensed nothing at all, is, as it is for all of us, quite idle speculation. According to plan, Frank and Percy arranged the funeral, since Henry had no children and no surviving relatives to perform the office. Henry was cremated after a short ceremony, with mourners who counted on the fingers of one hand. As Frank stood watching the curtains close and hearing the coffin sliding behind them, taking Henry on his final journey this side of eternity, he thought again of the things they had said to him on their last visit – the silly things, like going on a trip together when Henry's health improved.

But he knew there was something that they could not have told Henry, because it had already happened even before Henry had been admitted to hospital. Something had happened that ruled out such pathetic suggestions like 'When you're better we'll have a few pints in The Red Lion, and you can smoke your pipe …'. Had they said this, and had Henry heard and understood it, he would have known it to be a lie, albeit a lie that sprang from love, a love shrouded in a sense of sheer helplessness and despair.

8
Incitement to Social Incohesion

Henry would have known it to be a lie, because The Red Lion was not only smoke-free, but, for some time now, alcohol-free as well. 'It's just crazy!' Henry had said when the idea of alcohol-free pubs was first mooted in a government White Paper and had, quite understandably, been highlighted in the press. And the three friends had all agreed that the suggestion was insane and could not possibly go any further; they had also agreed that those responsible for the White Paper were fitting candidates for psychiatric treatment – though these were not quite the words they employed. The whole subject, as everyone in The Red Lion agreed, was simply an eccentric aberration and would very quickly be relegated to the nursery of political idiocy.

But, as history shows and as Percy knew full well, many a political idiocy finds its way into the statute books, despite the furore that might emanate from certain lowly quarters and commercial interests. Secular and religious factors had combined to make the eccentric not only feasible but, following a parliamentary vote, inevitable. Breweries, at least for the foreseeable future, were to continue to brew; and alcoholic products continued to be available in special outlets – but not in pubs, which were forbidden, on pain of immediate closure, to offer, or to stock alcohol of any kind. As for the special outlets, alcohol might be sold *on ration* only to those who had successfully applied for a licence to purchase; and the criteria on which such licences could be obtained included a spotless criminal record and driving licences so clean that they smelled of disinfectant. Custodial sentences for alcohol-fuelled crime were mandatory, not only for cases involving Manslaughter or Accidental Killing but also Grievous Bodily Harm; but such instances seemed to pass without much public disfavour in a context in which the return of the death penalty for capital crime was also now beginning not merely to be mooted, but to loom on the not-too-distant horizon. Meanwhile, the building of new prisons, now termed *rehabilitation centres*, was firmly on government agendas and promised a veritable archipelago of reformatory possibilities, not to say an improvement in employment figures and a boost to the economy.

For it was not simply a return to the Prohibition Era (or 'Error', as Percy once jibed). The prohibition of alcohol was only a strand in a much larger fabric; for the law under whose auspices alcohol was prohibited became known as the ISI, *Incitement to Social Incohesion*.

There had been calls to *simplify* the law, calls which were welcomed vociferously by well-meaning but simple-minded politicians, who believed that the interests of *ordinary* people would be better served by a rigorous application of Ockham's Razor, by pruning or cutting away the dense forests of legal terminology and reducing them to more manageable chunks; there was at first some confusion concerning whether *the law itself* should be so reduced or merely its *application*, but it was quickly and readily agreed that the distinction between the law itself and its application was a philosophical imponderable and should, like all philosophical imponderables, be ignored altogether. The spiny thickets of the law having been abandoned, laws touching Slander and Libel, for example, could be comfortably accommodated under the general heading *Incitement to Social Incohesion*. The scene was now set for glorious simplification under the comforting umbrella of ISI, with the delightful result that our much-vaunted common sense and the humanity of taking circumstances into account were neatly, or not so neatly, sacrificed on the altar of reductionism. So it was that the simplification of the law, like the simplification of language itself, emanated from a confusion of mind and an assumed clarity of purpose. No one now dared to teach the law *differences*. In all this there was something horrific; for the simplicity achieved was not to be confused with the simplicity of a virtuous life, or the simplicity in the face of one who loves unconditionally, or the simplicity of the childlike pleasures in which a simple life may consist, or the simplicity of childlike innocence, so rare and so coveted amongst the virtuous. In the simplification of language and of law there is no virtue.

'"Incohesion" – I'm not sure it's even a bloody word!' Percy complained, when the phrase began to acquire some currency. 'They've made it up! They've coined it!' The ISI became a blanket category, a catch-all; it was meant to cover a multitude of sins – and it did just that. As far as alcohol-limitation was concerned, this would not have worried 'good' Muslims and others of some minority creeds; it would have been welcomed by some Christians, those who had developed an outrageously excessive dislike of excess. But for the three friends and everyone else in The Red Lion, it was anathema to good sense and an affront to personal liberty. What were pubs, after all, if they were alcohol-free, and alcohol-free by force of law, to boot? Such was the prattle in The Red Lion and in every other pub in the land. But prattle, as any good dictionary will tell you, is no more than inconsequential talk. What was consequential was the law, for breaking it implied consequences too brutal to be contemplated. There were of course some spasmodic attempts to do more than simply prattle on about it; but public protests, in the form of marches or sit-downs, were very likely to erupt in violence, and violence, even when moderate, was easily subject to ISI, and a custodial sentence meant loss of earnings, even of jobs, and, what was worse, a criminal record; on balance, therefore, visible and unambiguous opposition was not considered to be worth the proverbial candle. What was particularly worrying was that the press was curiously muted about it all; at least, it was curious to those to whom such things are a disquieting curiosity; but, in the main, a muted press was passed over in corresponding silence. Outlets for protest were therefore either too dangerous or non-existent.

Such prattle was largely the result of pinpointing the particular and missing the general. Percy had his thoughts, which, for the moment, he tended to keep to himself. He and Frank both had bitterly resented the fact that they could not have promised Henry a puff and a pint, even if Henry could not possibly have survived to enjoy them. But Percy's reflections stretched wider than this. For the preservation of social cohesion seemed now to imply not only the loss of some of the simple pleasures of life, but the very bigotry which he had met with in his study of history, the very stuff he had been at pains to point out to his students; whether or not his students had listened, it had been important for Percy to make a stand and be counted, which he strove to do in the classroom , as much for his own sake as for that of the young people he addressed, who would be the citizens and the guardians of the future; but if these young people were to grow up in an aura of bigotry, history, with all its sins and horrors, could be expected to repeat itself. Homophobia, a case in point, had been increasing in recent years, and it was beginning to look as though the response from on high was to embrace rather than oppose it and that, therefore, the liberal and liberating legislation of the 1960s was in danger of repeal. Anti-Semitism was also on the up; and it seemed that political correctness, even if originally conceived to be a phenomenon designed to be fair to everybody, had turned out to be prejudicial, since it seemed that criticism of one particular faith, Islam, tended to be condemned, even without so much as a preliminary hearing, while criticism of any other tended to be overlooked. Percy was repeatedly haunted by his own words as they hammered away inside his head: *Yesterday, the day before yesterday, and all our yesterdays, are one –*

and today is tomorrow's yesterday. The horrors of history were on the march, as though they had never slept.

It really did seem that the rot had set in. It was just as well, for example, that the smuggling in of pipe tobacco for Henry had not been discovered; to have been caught in the act would have been seen to commit ISI; they would not have had a leg to stand on, for appeals to humanity, decency and a simple act of kindness, would never have gone down well with the *panel.* The panel for each county consisted of three magistrates, and no legal representative worth his salt would put his career on the line to take on cases whose only defence consisted in an appeal to humanitarian considerations, for such grounds were not now permissible in law. The ISI was not only a catch-all; it was also exclusively and mechanically legal, for it refused to 'take circumstances into account'.

'It's just a mess!' Percy blurted out one evening in The Red Lion. Mess or not, the ISI continued alive and well.

Frank and Percy still patronised The Red Lion, despite everything. And 'everything' included a change in proprietorship, for without a by-your-leave Malcolm had disappeared to no one knew where, his place being taken by a weedy sort of fellow called Harold, who served drinks at the bar in a very matter-of-fact kind of way, humourless and devoid of the customary chit-chat and social exchanges. Malcolm's departure was not unique; as if in sympathy, Wild Bill and The Yellow Rose of Texas ceased their patronage, perhaps to try pastures new, but there were no pastures different. The place had therefore become characterless and as featureless as a cold, tasteless jelly.

Frank and Percy sat at the same table and in the same positions; in fact, everything was the same in the very midst of difference, as the familiar might suddenly and strangely take on an unfamiliar, not to say hostile, aspect with the death of a loved one. They were experiencing the gradual chipping away of the familiar. They would sit, often in silence, clutching their unappetising glasses of mineral water or fruit juice; but Percy was a seething cauldron on the inside, and sometimes the expression on his face was suggestive of a volcanic eruption, an outburst in the making.

'It's just a damned obsession!' he said one evening. 'I mean, what have we come to? More to the point, what have we all allowed ourselves to come to?' Frank just shook his head slowly and thoughtfully. It was best not to say too much, anyway. The walls had ears, not to mention Harold's own, which seemed to stick out of either side of his head like cabbage-leaf antennae, poised and ready, it seemed, to detect anything that might conceivably be construed as a case of ISI.

Even if ISI had, in Percy's opinion, been in every way unobjectionable, he would still have claimed the right to question it, for to question was not necessarily to condemn. Percy was almost born with questions on his lips; even as a child he would roam the hills of his Midland town, hills man-made out of coal waste in the far off days when coal mining was not only a viable industry, but the mainstay occupation of the local community, to the extent that, without it, the local community would have collapsed altogether. Grass had eventually begun to grow on those black hills, and young Percy would sit atop of them in a posture of questioning, almost like a very junior Rodin's *Thinker*. Where had the hills come from? – and, were they going anywhere? What was *everything*? Where had everything come from? – and where was everything going? He would ask such questions as an imaginative child might ask them – in an aura of simple innocence and curiosity, no strings attached.

No, to question was not necessarily to condemn. But as Percy saw it, ISI was by no means in every way unobjectionable, and in particular because it involved the rape of language and of law itself.

For as the years passed and Percy's reflections had matured, he began to see that his natural curiosity meant nothing at all if it could not be continually enriched, and enrichment implied the ability to articulate, and articulation implied words; and all this had to do with the quality of one's journey through life; for it was not the destination of the journey that mattered, for the destination of life was the grave, and he had long been mindful of those lines of Donne: *The grave's a fine and quiet place, but none I think do there embrace.* Surely people understood the importance of the journey itself; though, judging by the faces he surveyed in buses and trains, it seemed that people were obsessed by their destinations. No matter, they would learn in time that destinations were of less account than the means taken to achieve them, just as someone had long ago pointed out that *being* was immensely more important than *doing*.

Percy had taken his cue from his first role model. But his first role model, subsequently to be bolstered by those in ancient halls of fame, was his history teacher. It was not what Mr John Andrews had said so much as what he had not said. Not so much his words as his whole approach and his mannerisms, and, above all, his genteel and interminable curiosity – this is what had taken root in Percy's own psyche. He and the other boys had made gentle fun of him at the time – the way he would walk slowly round the classroom stroking his cheek with the palm of his hand, beginning to say something, also slowly, and then checking himself with the words 'No, I'm being stupid', or 'No, no, that can't be right. Let me start again.' 'When Cromwell … No, let me put it another way …' was an in-joke amongst his pupils. When out of school, they would ape his movements, his slow drawl and his self-criticism, making each other rock with laughter. Mr Andrews was unique amongst his colleagues and, as Percy came to realise, was rare amongst men. His continual attempts to get things right, to be forever reasonable, struck a lasting chord with Percy. This was a man whose integrity was something to emulate, perhaps above all other things. His eccentricities did not matter. In fact, as Percy pondered the matter, his integrity was itself an eccentricity; after all, there would not be too many teachers who called themselves stupid in front of their pupils; it was far more likely that the epithet would be launched against pupils themselves, regardless of whether it did any lasting harm. Percy was inclined to think that people should talk not so much of the value of education as such, but of the value of educators; few people would remember the nuts and bolts of what they had been taught, but it was far more likely that they would remember, for good or for ill, those who had taught them. How facile, how wrong-headed, then, to speculate on the pros and cons of whether one day teachers would be replaced by robots. True, a robot might be a better option than a bad teacher; but it is better to have some bad teachers if this is the price we must pay for good ones. Without the good teachers, Henry had once agreed, on one of the nights in The Red Lion, 'It would be like going in at the front and going straight out the bloody back!' 'Like a garage without a mechanic,' Frank had chipped in. 'Well, a garage without a *good* mechanic, at any rate,' Percy had added.

All this stuff about social cohesion was just too much for a man like Percy and all his role models to stomach. What was going on was just over the top. If it was still his world, perhaps it was not now his time; if it was still his time, perhaps it was not now his world. Society had become too overtly dysfunctional for his liking.

No, Percy was not demented; not suffering from the senility that comes with age. Perhaps he was suffering from the confusion that comes with an overdose of integrity. As he looked round the world now, at faces on buses and trains, he saw that things, especially people, had changed and that his world, or the world he had known, was struggling to survive and would be remembered only on bric-a-brac stalls. Naturally, there was nothing new about change; nothing new about the discomfort that the elderly might feel towards it. But then, there is change and there is change, and not every change is for the better, just as there is power and there is power, for the power of love is not like the power that the strong wield over the weak or the power that refuses to brook questions let alone opposition. The power of love is what Henry had revealed from within himself, as he lay in bed falling in love with the faces of strangers; the power that emanated from Henry was neither hurtful nor destructive, unless, that is, it went with the false expectation that such love could possibly be returned. Henry had had no such expectation, and therefore was neither hurt nor destroyed by the power that resided within his own breast.

9
The Trial of Percy Fletcher

The irony was almost comic – the fact that Percy's initials also denoted Political Correctness, a concept which had started as a light aircraft and ended up on a journey to Saturn. Political Correctness had been elevated to a status which placed it very much under the auspices of *Incitement to Social Incohesion,* and now it was not only a question of having to watch one's p's and q's, out of considerations of simple decency and respect, but of receiving a mandatory custodial sentence on the slightest provocation. You had to be aware that people with a grudge might make an accusation against you which, however flimsy, however unfounded, even *false,* might land you in very hot water indeed. Mathew Hopkins, the self-styled Witchfinder General of the seventeenth century, would have delighted in the opportunities now provided by ISI, for all kinds of calumnies, falsehoods and reprisals might now find protection and patronage in the watchful eyes of the law.

And the eyes of the law were more watchful than ever before, a thought that could not help but strike Percy as he looked first straight ahead at the magistrate's bench and then up to the insignia of Justice that stood behind the three dignitaries employed by the state to administer the law impartially, without favour and devoid of malice.

The concept of impartiality had somehow taken a wrong turn on the journey to Saturn. Homophobia and anti-Semitism for example, had increased in recent years; but, instead of meeting them with a counteractive response under the aegis of political correctness, homosexuals and Jews were routinely subjected to abuse without any legal action being taken or so much as threatened; the law had taken a back seat in the matter – as though to appease the Muslim fraternity, those who had become known as *Orthodox* Christians, and those of some sundry other faiths, all of whom regarded homosexuality and Judaism as an irretrievable sin against a God who was perched on high and had donned an equally irretrievable frown. Therefore, political correctness, originally conceived, one dared to hope, to be fair to all and sundry, had in fact become most partial in application. Perhaps the route to Saturn was more zig than zag and involved two steps forward and one step back, if not one step forward and two steps back. In any case, the concept of impartiality had twisted out of shape.

Percy stood in the dock, still wondering how he had got there. In one sense, he knew very well, none better; in another, he did not. Because the whole thing was madness, utter madness! Alright, he might have said something in The Red Lion. He remembered his outburst one night, perhaps when the phoenix had at last managed to rise from the ashes and take flight. Things inside his head had come to a kind of climax. He said something about society going to pot, perhaps he had blamed it all on religion. Something about religion being primitive and those believing in it causing more trouble than they are worth; something as well about the rights of everyman, which included homosexuals and atheists; something about the warped nature of ISI. Moreover, he had made no bones about it, making sure that everyone could hear him, despite Frank's attempt to pacify him. 'Sssh, for God's sake!' Frank had whispered. But that only made matters worse. 'Don't talk to me about God!' Percy rejoined, before slamming into Islam and every other religion under the sun, including that of Old George Fox. There seemed to be no stopping him. He went on a critical spree. Soon he seemed to be bashing history, as well. 'I mean, why bother teaching it?' he said. 'Nobody ever learns from it; in fact, they don't need to *falsify* it, because they just *ignore* it. So why not just give up teaching it at all? Yes, that's right, *delete* history itself! What a splendid idea! Funny no one's ever thought of it. Such a simple idea, too. Well, they say that the best ideas are simple. The world is full of clever *idiots*. They say history is subjective – you can *never* get to the truth, according to them. Alright, then – I've got the perfect solution. Just give up teaching it altogether and make people like me redundant. How about that, Mr John Andrews? The civilised world *has no place* for the likes of *you*!' Percy's accentuated words punched through the air like barbed arrows as he darted glances round the pub, seeming to address its expressionless patrons as though they were an audience.

The proprietor gave him some meaningful looks, but the storm had to be ridden out. After all, he could hardly be told that he had had too much to drink.

The storm did subside, much to Frank's relief, and the buzz and hum of the pub resumed.

'You need to be careful, you know.'

'Oh, I *know*, Frank!' Percy replied reprovingly.

'I mean, you should *write* about it. I know you've got a lot to say. But why don't you write about it instead?' Frank suggested gently.

'Too late. No one will publish it,' Percy replied peremptorily.

For Frank, this seemed defeatist. For Percy it was an admission that freedom of expression, the freedom he had grown up taking for granted, was no longer achievable.

Yes, Percy knew full well why he was standing in the dock charged under *Incitement to Social Incohesion*. What he didn't know was how it could possibly happen that a light aircraft could be well on its way to Saturn. Hopefully, it would run out of fuel as it encircled the ringed planet and burn up en route to the surface, landing there in a cloud of ash. Meanwhile, Percy might aid its destruction by speaking out against it in the dock, his face turned towards the magistrates and the insignia of Justice that was perched above their heads. Had he been a Socrates or a Sir Thomas More, he might have had his say; but because justice in this respect had since taken a turn for the worse, Percy had no option but to hear the charges, corroborated by only one witness, the proprietor of The Red Lion, and to make his plea. He had been advised to plead guilty; to do otherwise would mean impugning the law and that would have cut no ice with the magistrates, who might then pronounce a more severe sentence. But after the plea had been entered there was nothing to be done but to sentence him. True, Percy did try initially to get something across with a 'But' here and a 'However' there; but the phrase 'Contempt of Court' served to cut him short, and Percy ended up having no say at all.

Percy was sentenced to a minimum six-week custodial sentence, without Right of Appeal, the actual length of sentence being conditional upon the findings of the RPO's (Rehabilitation Programme Operative) report. Which meant that the offence carried a minimum but not a maximum sentence. If the RPO's findings proved negative, Percy could expect to remain in custody until such time that they proved positive, the maximum possible sentence being therefore indeterminate.

Frank, however, was quite relieved, believing that it could easily have been much worse – which, of course, was true. Six weeks, thought Frank, would pass in no time. Granted, he mused, prison is the last place on earth for poor Percy, and at his age, too; no, Percy deserved to be rewarded and applauded, not *punished*: What have things come to? Even so, things are as they are, and we must simply make the best of them. No, it could easily have been worse: six weeks is better than six months, and infinitely better than six years. After all, he wouldn't be missing anything in The Red Lion; in fact, it would be better to avoid the place altogether from now on; they might somehow be able to get their hands on a bottle of this or that and drink at home; things had come to a pretty pass, no question about it, but if they were careful there might yet be some light at the end of the tunnel. It was a good thing Alison was no longer around to see all this. Had Alison been alive, would Percy have toned it all down, and perhaps avoided prison? This was one of many imponderables, but it was likely that events would still have taken the turn they did. Not that his feelings for Alison were ever indifferent. On the contrary, his marriage, like all marriages, had had its ups and downs, but if a man's feelings are to be judged by how he reacts to loss, Percy's retreat into his books and his association with his two friends seemed to be all there was preventing him from cracking up altogether when Alison passed on. What *would* she say now? Frank was certain that she would never chide him for it or talk him down; she would be a rock – just as Sal had been to Frank. But this was no place for 'ifs' and 'buts', and 'what ifs' and 'woulds'. No, the whole thing must be faced squarely, and dealt with. There was nothing else for it – anything else was just asking for trouble.

Such was Frank's common-sense approach to matters.

So it was that Percy found himself incarcerated with people who had as much idea of Socrates or Sir Thomas More as the Man in the Moon. In fact, they were far better acquainted with the latter than the former, for the latter might be imagined as a possibility, however fanciful, however absurd, however childlike; but no one could even begin to put a face to Socrates or More, and it would not have mattered in the slightest if they could. It was one thing to imagine a man in the moon, quite another to imagine giving up your life, or, for that matter, anything at all of value to you, unless there was something in it for yourself; and there could not possibly be anything in it for you if you gave up your own life for it. Percy was in the company of people whom history had passed by; he found ample scope for agreeing with his own pronouncement that history might as well be deleted altogether. And if history were given up altogether, it would mean an enormous saving of resources, of time, of energy, and, in particular, of money, for, as everyone, even a dunce, would agree, time is money. Nor would he be likely to find anyone remotely interested in the trials and tribulations of a man like George Fox – a man who, like many of these inmates, had spent more time in prison than out of it, and all for the sake of religious conscience. 'Religious conscience' was not a phrase that burned on the lips of most people; about 'religious' most people had some vague idea, but 'conscience' was more slippery, and if you put these two words together, you would have lost your audience entirely; the phrase might have meant something in the past, but what on earth could it mean now? And for those few who knew a thing or two, the phrase 'religious conscience' was a milder alternative to 'religious bigotry' and was therefore derisory. Percy's conclusion was that when you speak to most people, it would be better to leave the word 'religious' out altogether.

Discussing his historical role models with his fellow inmates seemed out of the question; but he would fare no better with the warders and others involved in the lower strata of administration. For they knew as little and cared as little as the inmates themselves. Any expectations Percy might have entertained to the contrary were soon to be shattered into irreparable fragments.

Percy's rehabilitation programme consisted of two hour-long sessions a week for the first three weeks, followed by a one-hour session a week for the last three weeks, on the assumption that more time might be required in the first half of the sentence than in the second. These recorded sessions were meant to be anything but heart-to-heart; they were intended to allow inmates to get things off their chests and gradually to run down, rather like a battery in a toy clown. Each case would then be decided on its merits. If, as expected, every shred of incitement to social cohesion was dissipated, inmates might expect a timely release; were there doubts, however, as to their sincerity or future behaviour, weeks were added on; in the most stubborn of cases, prolonged sentences and loss of all privileges, amongst which were counted the withdrawal of hot meals, visits and daily exercise, would follow until the inmate fully understood on which side his bread was buttered. There were calls from both within and without the rehabilitation centres that stricter forms of treatment should be considered in the most stubborn cases, for faster and more effective results would take some of the pressure off a burgeoning rehabilitation centre population. Requests for writing materials, but not computers, were invariably met; they were considered to be a most useful indication of an inmate's progress; anything written would be collected and considered by the RPO, and would either go towards meeting, or extending, the planned release date. Percy was quick to take advantage of every opportunity to spell out his position; though eventually he came to see that it was better to write nothing at all if lying was not a route one felt morally capable of taking.

Percy welcomed the prospect of the first session with the RPO; he saw it as an opportunity to state his case, put forward his point of view, so that they would know where he was coming from. *Who knows?* he found himself thinking. *They might even reconsider!* He did not sound convincing, even to himself.

The RPO turned out to be a portly fellow in his mid-forties, clean-shaven, in a blue uniform – and a peaked cap, which he removed on entering the room and hung on a hook behind the door. Percy had already been brought to the Interview Room and was sitting at the large oaken table. For what seemed an age they both sat in silence across from one another while the RPO flicked through what Percy assumed was a file concerning the case. At length, the RPO closed the file and stared across at Percy.

'So, you know why you're here,' said the RPO. It was a statement, not a question. He was expressionless and his tone flat – all part of his training.

'As a matter of fact, I don't. But—'

'Neither do I,' interrupted the RPO. The RPO was good at interrupting; that was part of his training, too.

'Now, what *would* she say? Your wife – *Alison*, wasn't it?' For a moment the RPO sounded like Frank, who had asked him the same question before Percy went to court. The RPO's tone had suddenly changed to something distinctly more avuncular, as though he were a member of Percy's family and was putting Percy's interests first and his own very much in the background. The RPO knew his trade. But it wasn't Frank. No, it wasn't Frank at all, and it wasn't meant in the same way although the words of which it consisted were identical. There was something in the tone that made it sinister and painful. The question was not really relevant, anyway. But how could something so irrelevant also be so painful. He had no right to bring Alison into it. It was also patronising and belittling. All this went through Percy's mind, but too quickly to articulate properly, and in any case the RPO would give no credit for articulation.

'She passed away,' Percy found himself saying, weakly.

'What *would* she say?' the RPO repeated, again in a familiar tone and as though Percy had said nothing. 'And at your time of life, too,' the RPO added, as though an afterthought.

Percy was silent. To have responded as though it were a question well-meant would have given both it and the RPO credit which neither deserved. They sat in silence for a few moments as the RPO scrutinised him; Percy thought he saw a flicker of a smile on his lips, but all doubt was removed when the RPO spoke again, returning to his 'official' tones.

'Would you like to tell me something? I believe you have something to tell me – about why you think you are here, in this place, locked up!' Perhaps this was the cue Percy had been waiting for; what he was not allowed to say in court he could now attempt to deliver at length. Before the interview he had worked it all out. He wanted to say that it was all a misunderstanding. But a misunderstanding about *what* exactly? It was very important to be clear about this, because he could not argue that it was a misunderstanding about ISI – it was like a game, because if you accepted the rules, you could play the game, and ISI was the Rule Book; Percy had broken the rules, and therefore he had to face the music. Yes, but supposing you wanted to challenge the Rule Book *itself*? Well, if you challenged the rules, you would be challenging the game, because the rules define the game; in this case, he would be challenging ISI, and that meant questioning the law and the authority behind it. It would be like challenging the jurisdiction of the court; if the law was wrong, then anything it encompassed or implied, like his own incarceration and even the interview with the RPO, was founded on error. He would be refusing to acknowledge the rightness of the law; he would be refusing to play the game. It would be like arguing against car travel as you sat next to the driving instructor in your first driving lesson: 'You must turn the key in the ignition to start the engine—' 'Yes, but why bother to start the engine at all? I mean, why bother to make the car move?' What could a driving instructor do with responses like this? He might invite you to get out of the car, his time, and your money, having been wasted.

Percy had concluded that it was impossible to state his case without at the same time impugning the law itself, for it was not a simple question of having to question the facts or the circumstances of the case; after all, he had already pleaded guilty. In terms of the law, he *was* guilty. Well, if he was obliged to impugn the law, then so be it; either that, or sit there in silence and play stupid, and he was determined not to do that.

'She would have stuck by me,' Percy said.

'What was that?'

'I said, she – Alison, my wife – would have supported me.' A few moments' silence followed. Should he start with George Fox, who refused to subscribe to the Oath of Allegiance to Charles II simply because he believed it unchristian to make any oaths at all, although he meant no disrespect, let alone harm, to the king? And although he had offered instead to make a declaration of support *in lieu*? But in refusing to take the oath he was breaking the law, and was therefore subject to a custodial sentence. Or was it better to start with Sir Thomas More, who had said 'I do none harm, I say none harm, I think none harm, and if that is not enough to keep a man alive, then in truth I have no wish to live'? Or should he begin with Socrates, who, facing trumped-up charges in a hostile court, had suggested that he should be rewarded with a fat pension for his troubles.

Percy had already decided to abandon the name-dropping, which would only have confused the RPO, who had in all likelihood never heard of them anyway, and simply appeal to everyone's democratic right, in a *genuine* democracy, to question and to think and speak critically, provided that such freedom is exercised without malice and in a spirit of equally *genuine* inquiry. After all, Thomas More himself had said that without malice there can be no harm.

'The fact is,' began Percy, trying very hard not to sound professorial, 'I think things have gone pear-shaped – you know what I mean? You see, everybody has a right in our society to question and criticise. All I did was to exercise that right – and for that I've landed myself in prison'.

'This is a *Rehabilitation Centre*!' the RPO corrected him in stern tones.

'Well, whatever you call it. And it's not right. Not right at all. History teaches us time and again—'

'Time for tea, I'd say,' said the RPO, stopping Percy short.

'What?' Percy smiled, bemused by what he thought he had heard.

'Tea-time. Time for tea. You understand that, don't you? Oh, no – not *here*. You can have a cup of tea brought to your cell – I mean, *room*.'

This signalled the end of the first session with the RPO. Percy was led back to his room.

Percy had a lot to think about. He sat in his sparsely furnished room thinking of what should happen next, and in the next session with the RPO. What was the point saying anything at all? Whatever he said seemed to make either the wrong impression or no impression at all.

When the second session came round, Percy was obviously more guarded. They sat once again at the same table, and after a few moments silence, the RPO piped up:

'Well, you look a bit glum!'

'Do I, indeed?'

'You should know we have a duty of care towards you. We – all of us here – we're looking after your interests. I hope you know that.'

'I don't know anything of the kind.' The phrase 'duty of care' did not impress Percy. Like 'political correctness', it might have started off on the right foot, but it had hitched a ride on the rocket to Saturn and was now encircling the planet and threatened to go even further into space. It was just another instance of how words became phrases and phrases became clichés and clichés became snares to trap the innocent along with the guilty. Words simply start as groups of letters, but they can turn blood-red on the lips of beasts; like the obscenity of the word 'Comrade' in the mouth of a brute.

'You shouldn't be afraid to speak. We're all here to help you.'

'I'm not afraid.'

The silence was uncomfortable, even for the RPO. Silence is a phenomenon that has been remarked upon, both by the malicious and by the compassionate, as a difficult ambiguity. Percy was silent. Was this a confession of the error of his ways? Or was it a confirmation of guilt. It was time to find out.

'Well, then. You said something last time about freedom. Freedom implies responsibility, doesn't it? Incitement is a serious matter.'

'I didn't *incite* anyone.'

'Well, it's just a word. Shall we say *encourage* then?'

'I didn't *incite* and I didn't *encourage*. I just exercised my right as a free citizen in a democratic society. I said what I thought. It's a question of live and let live, but, as John Stuart Mill said—'

'Tea?'

*   *

In subsequent sessions, Percy sat silent. On one occasion he simply said, 'Not guilty,' and the RPO simply responded with, 'But you pleaded guilty, and it's too late to change your plea.'

The RPO's report repeatedly employed the adjectives 'uncooperative', 'inflexible' and 'unrepentant', and the prospects were looking increasingly bleak for Percy's initial release date. In his first visit, Frank had appealed to Percy to say or do anything within reason to cooperate, just to secure the earliest possible release. But Percy seemed determined to out-Pickwick Mr Pickwick in his obstinate refusal to satisfy the demands of wrong over right. As Percy saw it, Might was not Right and never could be Right; it was not just a question of the definition of words but of the definition of his whole life. He could not possibly backtrack on everything he had attempted to instil into his pupils; it would be like admitting that a lifetime of pointing to the lessons of history had been entirely meaningless. After all, what was the use in extolling the virtues of his role models if he was not prepared to live up to them? What was virtue without courage? He was certain that Alison would agree if she could. He had come this far; if he should go back on everything he had taught, on everything he had learned, he would not be able to look himself in the face again. He understood Thomas More far better now. Admittedly, he might have lacked courage had Alison been alive; he would have been bound to take her into account, and therefore to consider his job. James Naylor, Quaker and associate of George Fox, had probably been in the same position before his own Damascus conversion when:

> I began to make some preparation, as apparel and other necessaries, not knowing whither I should go, but, shortly afterwards, going agateward with a friend from my own house, having on an old suit, without any money, having neither taken leave of wife or children, not thinking then of any journey, I was commanded to go into the west, not knowing whither I should go, nor what I was to do there, but, when I had been there a little while, I had given me what I was to declare, and ever since I have remained not knowing today what I was to do tomorrow.

And all this because Naylor had been given the promise that God would be with him, 'Which promise I find made good every day.'

Percy would have admitted that he lacked the courage of Naylor's religious convictions to leave everything and everyone behind, and he sometimes wondered whether it was courage or something less virtuous. But he was more than prepared to give rare people like Naylor the benefit of the doubt.

In any case, Alison was no more, except perhaps in spirit, and that spirit, he felt sure, was perfectly in tandem with his own. Freed from more worldly responsibilities, it was very much a case of in for a penny, in for a pound. He might as well be hanged for a sheep as for a lamb. It was all the way now. Not that he would be hanged; things had come to a pretty pass, but not *that* pretty – not yet, at any rate. No, the fact is that he had lived his life and done his job with the usual panoply of constraints; they were necessary for survival; as a teacher he could push the limits in the classroom, but only so far; school inspections and doting parents had ideas of their own, not necessarily shared by Percy; but he had to be mindful of them. However, circumstances had now changed and he felt like a free man despite the fact that he was now incarcerated. The irony was almost amusing. *Almost.* He was not perfect in everything he said and did. But he knew that perfection is not to be confused with infallibility: perfection is not the absence of error, any more than courage is the absence of fear; no, perfection is not the absence of mistakes, but the desire not to make them, or to make as few as possible. He was determined now not to make more mistakes than he had already made. Had he been of a deeply religious cast of mind, like James Naylor, he would have thought that his whole life might now be vindicated if he could hear the voice of God at last before having to shake off this mortal coil. He was no James Naylor. Neither was he a George Fox; but he admired George Fox, perhaps before all other men, for his staggering integrity, for his boundless humanity and courage, and his apparently infinite capacity for suffering. In the words, if not with the religious conviction, of George Fox, Percy would have accepted the mission: *Let all nations hear the word by sound or writing. Spare no place, spare not tongue nor pen; but be obedient to the Lord God and go through the work and be valiant for the Truth upon earth.*

Percy was determined to speak his mind. And he would spare no place, either. He began with his cellmate, one Charlie Dobson, whose offence consisted in repeatedly smoking in public places. Charlie had left school at sixteen and was now in his mid-thirties. All things considered, Charlie should have been credited with the patience (or was it bewilderment?) to listen so patiently as Percy began to extol the virtues of a free society. But almost as soon as he started Percy realised he was speaking largely to himself, and poor Charlie thought the whole exercise centred on the right to smoke where, when and as you like, and nothing more. Percy was interrupted mid-stream by the question, 'Do you smoke, then?' and felt quite deflated. When Percy tried to drag Thomas More into the lesson, Charlie wondered how many *he* had smoked and whether or not he had inhaled. No, no, it was quite hopeless. As Charlie saw it, Percy was as eccentric as they come and had probably been incarcerated in the interests of the saner members of society, as a public nuisance. Charlie would have to try to put up with him; but he was greatly relieved when Percy soon stopped talking about whatever he was talking about, and peace reigned supreme again in the cell. Needless to say, word soon spread amongst the inmates that Percy was some kind of mad professor who had been detained for the public good.

But if speaking was so evidently pointless, he would write instead. 'Spare not tongue nor pen,' Old George had said. He poured out his 'incitements' on paper. He realised, of course, that the stuff would be taken away and read; but that was precisely what he wanted to happen. Would there be someone somewhere in the system who might with some luck understand what he was driving at? Percy entertained the thought; it flew through his mind like a dart through gossamer, not daring to be held and scrutinised; he knew full well that this was a case of hopelessly wishful thinking. Such thoughts abandoned, the idea occurred to him that he might be able to smuggle out his scribbling during Frank's next visit. He needed to act fast for it was looking very much as if these visits would be terminated; such privileges were withdrawn in 'difficult' cases as a further incentive to cooperate. It did not occur to him until he was halfway through that Frank would be searched on the way out and that Frank would himself be landed in hot water for aiding and abetting dissidence. Well, he would write anyway.

'Well, this is a fine mess,' said Frank, sounding a bit like Oliver Hardy.

Percy just shrugged his shoulders and made a gesture with his hands, as if to say, 'Well, that's how the cookie crumbles.'

'Yes, but this is no way to spend your retirement. I mean it's just …' Frank didn't finish his sentence and just shook his head slowly from side to side.

Silence.

'Nothing to lose,' said Percy at last.

'Rubbish!'

Silence. Percy shrugged again.

'You're a good friend. Just go, Frank. Go home. It'll be fine.'

There really was nothing to say. Nothing at all. It was almost like the way it had been when they had both visited Henry in hospital before Henry passed silently away. Words were pointless now, as pointless as they were with Charlie or with the RPO or with the magistrates. Words were all there were. Yet they were pointless, like a gun without ammunition, a recipe without ingredients, a fishing rod without bait, a pipe without tobacco. You could admire their form, but they did no real work; they just went round and round, like a cog that fails to engage, like a paper plane that fails to make it to the other side of the room.

10
And Then There Was One

Time passed, but there was no time for further sessions with the RPO.

Percy had never had a strong physical constitution; even as a child he became breathless on the playing field long before half-time, and was often glad, though somewhat embarrassed, to deliver a *Please-excuse-him* note to the PE teacher. Sports and similar animations were never for him, which was a pity since he carried his weak constitution with him into old age, though, by now, approaching your mid-seventies was not considered 'old' – perhaps again just a question of words. Be that as it may, his constitution, together with the trials and tribulations common to most people, amongst which the loss of Alison was undoubtedly the heaviest to bear, and in more recent years the decline, as he saw it, of civilisation itself, with the restraints and constraints imposed upon it by the needless, not to say cruel and mindless, impositions of which he himself had now fallen victim – all this seemed to conspire together to weaken him physically, just as much as his resolve to gets things off his chest seemed to strengthen him spiritually. This was a sad and unwanted irony. His physical strength was deserting him when he needed it most. And in this, it was not simply his lack of religious conviction that distinguished him from George Fox, the man who had held a lasting fascination over him, for Fox had the physical constitution of the proverbial ox, which had stood him in good stead for all the persecution that awaited him from the ungodly and the godly alike. Fox and ox had combined to face the world with the awesome task of telling it how things really stood. What Percy had lacked in physical stamina, Alison had made up for in myriad forms of support; in her absence Percy was left very much to his own devices and his dwindling reserves of energy, a condition to which his poor diet had contributed and an amelioration of which the Rehabilitation Centre could not be expected to furnish. It was now very much a case of what happens when an irresistible force meets an immoveable object, and it would be amusing but useless to try to decide whether Percy was the former or the latter in this formidable duo. We may be satisfied with the reflection that something, somehow, somewhere had to give.

And so it certainly did.

The first indications of the beginning of the end for Percy occurred while he was busy scribbling away at what he now regarded as no more than a little personal therapy or even a way of killing time. It has been fairly remarked that fact is often stranger than fiction, a truth which has something to do with the many ironies of life, and there was much irony in Percy's decline, though there were few that would have been capable of understanding it, even if his scribbling had lasted the course. As an example of the tenacity of a virtuous soul, and perhaps here he was also thinking of George Fox, not to mention himself, he decided to write something about the trial of Socrates. He chose to refer to that part of Plato's *Apology* in which Socrates, on trial for his life, meditates on the nature of death in what was, one may presume, a packed courtroom. The question Socrates discusses is whether death is a kind of dreamless sleep, as some believe it to be, or whether it is a transition to an afterlife, as others would prefer it to be. The conclusion Socrates reaches is that either way death is a boon, something to be looked forward to; the corollary, one supposes, is that to be *threatened* with it is a misunderstanding. And this is a dig at his judges, who are determined to put an end to him once and for all; if it is an eternal and dreamless sleep, there is nothing to fear; if it is a transition to another life, he would simply continue to question those he meets there as he has questioned those in this life; either way, he is unafraid and totally unrepentant.

As Percy continued to scribble away, somewhat amazed and uncommonly pleased with his own fluency, his right hand, which held the pen, seemed to slip away from the paper, as if controlled by someone or something else; he tried to bring it back to the paper, but it refused to obey him. Percy slumped into his chair, unable to call for help, let alone move. As if to mock him, his little remaining luck was that, a few moments later, a warder glimpsed him through the small window in the door and detected that something was not right, the expression on Percy's face being fixed and misshapen and his whole posture being strangely deranged.

Frank found him in a hospital bed looking very unlike himself, his mouth a little twisted, his features not exactly contorted but curiously unfamiliar in a way Frank was unable to fathom, his skin grey. He blinked a greeting as Frank brought a chair closer to the bed.

'He finds it difficult to speak – but he can understand you alright,' said a young nurse, just the sort of nurse that Henry would have fallen for without reservation, thought Frank later. Percy motioned, as best he could, with his left arm, to the bedside table on his left.

'Oh, he wants you to have that envelope. I put your name on it for him, but he wrote the note inside, with his left hand, too. Wasn't easy for him – I mean, just in case you're wondering.' She handed Frank the envelope.

'Right. I'll open it later, shall I? Percy?' Percy blinked an affirmative.

'Well, how is he, nurse? I mean, when ...'

'He's had a nasty stroke, haven't you Percy?' the young nurse said caringly. 'It's going to take time. We'll all have to be very patient, won't we Percy? No football for you for a while!'

'Plenty of rest,' Frank put in.

'That's right. That's absolutely right. In fact, it's a bit too early for visitors, really.'

'Yes, well, they said I could see him. No relatives, you see. But I take your point. Yes, I think I should go now, Percy – give you a chance. Yes?'

It was time to go even before Frank had tried to settle into that hard hospital chair. And this kind of one-sided, almost patronising, conversation, with its unbearable moments of silence was difficult – as difficult as it was later to recall. Frank called to mind how he and Percy had struggled to keep a falsely light conversation going when Henry was beginning to sink. But, of course, Frank had had to come. He was right that Percy had no relatives; Alison and he had fostered two boys, being unable to have children of their own, but they had lost touch with them years ago, and since Alison's passing nothing seemed to matter any more; the old world had gone, and the new was a most unsatisfactory replacement.

Frank got up from the chair and, as he did so, Percy, with some considerable effort, nodded towards the envelope Frank held in his hand.

'Yes, yes, old chap. I've got it. I'll read it.' Percy blinked in reply, as Frank put the envelope in the inside pocket of his jacket and patted it firmly.

'Right,' said Frank, as he turned in the doorway to face Percy, 'I'll see you again, soon. And no jumping out of bed in the meantime! Soon, old chap!'

And that was that. But how strange it was to be talking *at* Percy rather than *with* him, as though Percy had become a kind of hologram. Well, he was certainly a shadow of his former self. Yes, but it *was* Percy, all the same, and the change was pitiful. Poor Percy, thought Frank, who had got himself banged up in prison and was now down with a stroke. Percy was certainly more sinned against than sinning, but, with any luck, he might yet survive these ordeals.

And, in fact, it was just as well that the conversation had been difficult and one-sided and that the whole visit had been cut short. Otherwise, there was a risk either that Percy would have asked about The Red Lion or that Frank would have brought up the subject himself, and then Percy would have been most upset. A bulldozer had already turned up to reduce the old place to rubble, and this was not the time to relay such things to Percy. Memories, especially at a time like this, were precious and should be preserved – preserved against the onslaughts of time and circumstance. Thank goodness Frank had not forgotten himself and blurted anything out – which might easily have happened during one of those awkward silences when one is struggling to think of something to say, something, *anything*.

Hope might spring eternal, but human beings do not. Frank hoped that Percy would recover, or recover sufficiently at least to remain a companion as they both wended their ways through life and faced whatever life still had in store for them, and, he further hoped, that store would at least contain some small comforts, some little blessings that they might enjoy together.

Nevertheless, that awkward one-sided conversation was the very last thing they would share together. Percy suffered a further stroke and a massive brain haemorrhage, and parted this life during a dreamless night. Frank, as his only friend, and, officially, his most obvious contact, took it upon himself to make all the necessary arrangements, using Percy's life assurance as Percy had long intended in the event that he should be the first to shake off this mortal coil.

About Percy's funeral, the less said the better, which is precisely how Frank felt about it, since he was the only mourner, apart, that is, from the priest, who belonged, he said, to an independent church, though it could not have mattered less to Frank which church he belonged to or whether he belonged to any church at all. Frank said a few words before the coffin disappeared behind the screen, and felt rather silly in the process, for he felt as though he were speaking to himself, or as though he were simply going through the motions because that was the usual expectation – and Percy would not have approved. Frank remembered how Percy used to go on about the importance of words, and how words could come from the heart, or be directed, like arrows, to it, or how they could be meaningless in the mouths of those who used them, or how they could become, from humble beginnings, cruel barbs in the all-too-capable mouths of brutes. Of course, Frank meant the few simple words he said – about friendship and how Percy would be so badly missed – but he was upset by the inadequacy of these words, by the inadequacy of *all* words; how sad it was, this thought, when all we have left is words! He was, however, consoled by the idea, once explained by Percy himself, that it was not in such cases the words themselves that mattered but the feelings that gave rise to them, even when, as so often happens, only the words can be heard while the feelings that give vent to them are mute. It was the spirit of the thing that counted, according to Percy; and this was Percy's legacy from his understanding of George Fox who had, apparently, said the same sort of thing about the words of Scripture – that it was not the words that were holy, but the spirit from which they had sprung.

Be that as it may, Frank was much relieved when the funeral was over. 'I'm so glad it's over,' he said to himself, smiling as he imagined that Percy himself was saying the very same thing: 'Yes, me too!'

The joke fell limp, however, almost as soon as it was thought of. Because Frank was now on his own; the last of the Three Musketeers; the last of the Old Guard; the Last Man Standing – and that was not at all amusing. That was the terrible thing about death – it took away everything a man had by taking away his life, but it also robbed the living of the best things they had by taking away those they love; a double blow, so to speak. And it wasn't fair. It wasn't fair at all.

Such were Frank's ruminations as he made his way home from the funeral: another life gone; another life ruined. He would try to make the best of it; but making the best of it might not be good enough. What was this expression, anyway? – 'making the best of it'; words, just words again. A cliché, and one that is meant to help. But if the spirit behind words is the important thing, what is the spirit behind 'making the best of it' when you have lost someone so close to you, when there is no best to make anything of? Such thoughts were too much for Frank; thinking was made up of words, anyway; you couldn't escape from words; you were stuck with them. Perhaps silence is better, but silence makes you think, and thinking brings you face to face with words again; silence is hell, and perhaps noise is our escape route; the noise of sound, of music, of traffic – and of words!

Having made a cup of tea, Frank sat down in his favourite armchair, and, as he did so, the envelope, until now forgotten in the inside pocket of his jacket, reminded him of its existence. He took it out and, without opening it, laid it on the coffee table in front of him. 'For Mr Frank' it said in large letters on the front. He was amused by this form of address, but then he remembered that the nurse had written it and that she had spoken with an accent despite her fluent English. Frank was in no hurry to open it. As a matter of fact, he more than half wished that Percy had not written it at all. What was it, anyway? Poor Percy. He probably wanted to say his goodbyes, something nice – or perhaps something garbled and confused – although the nurse had said nothing to indicate that his mental state had been adversely affected. And then Frank remembered how worried he and Henry had been about Percy's mental wellbeing and how they had wondered whether or not he was suffering from – what do they call it? – oh yes, *early onset dementia*, or something like that. Well, it was all history now, all water under the bridge – but it would have been nice to have Henry there, to recall their mutual concern and wonder about the contents of that envelope.

'I wonder …' Frank began to say to himself, and then he checked the envelope. 'Yes, it is.' The envelope was properly stuck down. But the nurse had probably done that. Being properly stuck down was something of a relief, for it would take an effort to open. Had it not been stuck down, there would have been little excuse for further delay. Because it should, after all, be opened with the same care as it had been stuck down. To open it properly Frank would need to go into the kitchen and get a sharp knife in order to make a clean cut, that was only fair and respectful to Percy. For the time being, however, he was quite content to leave the envelope where he had replaced it – there, on the coffee table. There it would sit until he decided to make another cup of tea, necessitating a further trip into the kitchen, and then he could bring back a sharp knife and open the envelope properly. It took a considerable time for Frank to finish that cup of tea and then decide to have another; in fact, it was without doubt the longest cup of tea that Frank, or indeed in all probability anyone else, had ever had. But it finally and ceremoniously came to an end, and with it the excuse and the delay.

Frank shuffled back from the kitchen with a fresh cup of tea, having left behind his walking stick, which he now tended to use habitually, even at home. And then, having retrieved his walking stick and having placed it carefully to one side of his armchair so as not to knock over the second cup of tea, which he had placed with equal care on the coffee table, Frank settled down in his armchair, leaned gently forward and picked up the envelope.

11
The Conundrum

Frank slowly took the piece of paper from inside and, replacing the envelope on the coffee table, gently unfolded it as though it were a delicate and ancient artefact that predated recorded history. He opened it out, and there, in Percy's left-handed scrawl, was the verse:

Mary had a little lamb
Whose fleece was white as snow,
And everywhere that Mary went
The lamb was sure to go.

Frank was certainly puzzled, but could not have said, had he been asked, whether he was disappointed. The handwriting was not what you would have normally expected from Percy; but then, the poor fellow was obliged to use his left hand, and, as far as Frank could remember, Percy was right-handed. The childish scrawl was perfectly, and sadly, explicable. But what was unaccountable, and worryingly so, was that what Percy had written was equally childish. And then, in a flash, everything was clear. His stroke had obviously affected Percy's brain, and the poor fellow probably hadn't much idea of what or why he was scribbling; but perhaps he had just a vague idea that he was saying something to Frank, if, in fact, he had recognised Frank at all on Frank's last visit. Frank decided that the scribble was a product of poor Percy's physical and mental decline. But it was the last communication from the dear old chap and, as such, it deserved to be kept and kept safely. Frank respectfully folded the paper again, replaced it in its envelope and put the envelope in a drawer in his little desk. And there it would remain.

* *

Time passed, bringing with it decline, and yet further decline. Frank was finally obliged to use a wheelchair to get around and soon became wheelchair-bound. For the young, time may pass with indifference; for the lonely and the old and those constrained by the weaknesses of age, it may pass on crutches, as though in sympathy. Frank needed to employ a carer in order to remain at home and avoid the indignities he associated with care homes. The carer he employed was a middle-aged woman, and rather brusque and military in manner, but she got the domestic chores done with the minimum of fuss and Frank was inclined to forgive her for not being much of a conversationalist. Luckily, Frank did not need to rely on Mrs Slater for conversation.

Young Markus was ready and willing to take Frank out and about in his wheelchair, and was capable of supplying the kind of conversation Frank needed. Markus Shelby had recently received his doctorate in mathematics and was uncertain what to do with it; meanwhile, he was happy to do voluntary work, and that is how Frank made his acquaintance, on the unexpected recommendation of his brusque carer.

As Frank sat in his wheelchair at home, with Mrs Slater buzzing around the kitchen behind him, he could do little more, as he waited for Markus to call round, than to think through the life he had lived. Markus would call at any minute, and thoughts jumped into Frank's head – thoughts that were once crazy, especially when Percy had expressed them, but which now seemed only half as mad as they were. The thought, for example, that victory and defeat in war have exactly the same result, so that to speak of the *futility* of war would take on a new significance. It all had to do with all that stuff about continuity that Percy used to ramble on about – the way that you can never really destroy the evil that you seek to destroy in a *just* war, because it will always come back again, like persistent weeds in even the best kept of gardens. So, what's the point digging them up? But, no. No, of course not. There is every point digging them up – it's just that, when you think you've done the job, they pop up again. Perhaps a different variety of weed and in a different place in the garden – but weeds nonetheless. Dreadful, sobering continuity.

But his thoughts were also less abstract; thoughts about the things he had done and the things he had left undone. There was that little affair, for example, which really didn't amount to anything at all. It was just a solitary, transitory, *ever so* transitory, blip in his relationship with Sal. Even so, he wished Sal was there to apologise to, again, again, and again. He felt the need to apologise, to use *words*, for words were the conveyors of feeling – in this instance, regret. There was nothing to lose any more; it was time for openness, to put the cards on the table, to express his shame, his regret. There was no one there to apologise to, and yet her not being there made apology possible, because he could not fear losing her if she were not there. Courage by default, one might call it. In any case, courage too late. Alas, the fate of all old men is the irrepressible weight of memory; of memories good or bad, for even pleasant memories are bitter-sweet; the better they are, the more bitter-sweet.

Time passed slowly, but its effects were all too visible. Frank would stare at his hands – no longer smooth, well-toned and without blemish, as he *thought* he remembered them – for, after all, how many young men take cognisance of their hands? Now loose skin covered his fingers like a winding sheet on a corpse, and the backs of his hands were covered in large brown blotches as though he had been painting carelessly. His hands, which he could not now fail to notice, had become eminently visible reminders of his own mortality.

From his wheelchair he would look out the window and mark the seasons as they changed. He would ask himself which season he liked best. Why, spring, of course – the beginning of new life and … Yet, perhaps not so. There was something about every season, something to commend each one, and Frank would ponder on what it was that made each one commendable. Not winter, surely! Certainly not for the old who twitch with the cold and worry how to pay the heating bills. Yet reflections on the seasons would help him recall younger days, days when twitching with the cold was a far more remote possibility, days, even, when he positively relished the cold and looked forward to the snow and the silence it would bring; silence, an indescribable silence, especially up on the hills which he would roam as a child and which the snow would cover like a magic blanket – *deep, and crisp and even*, just as it had been when Good King Wenceslas looked out and spied *yonder peasant* in the days when alms were given to the poor; days which, to Frank's mind, contrasted with the present, in which nothing was given to anyone, except rules and all kinds of stringencies. The thought flashed through his mind that Percy would have something to say about the continuity of it all – the fact that the hardness of life in medieval England was hardly different from what it was now – no, not as it was in Frank's childhood, but as it had become and was now. And … but the thought was not held. Instead, he continued to think of the seasons and compared the silence of the snow-covered hills with the warm, silent stillness of summer when only the skylarks and the occasional bleats of sheep broke the unmoving air.

Memories were not the only bitter-sweet companions of Frank's constrained existence. He found a sad comfort in music, and would sit and listen to Bach as that angel of sound whisked him away on a musical journey, with its moving cadences, its rise and fall, its twists and turns, and returned him feeling as though he had been to another planet, a planet on which man's inhumanities to man were unknown and where energy was devoted to loving creation and not the instruments of war. Not that Frank could have given you a note-by-note analysis of a Bach suite; but he knew what he liked, and he knew what was good; his appreciation of music was, for want of a better word, *instinctive*; somehow, he did not know how, beauty contained within it its own validation, and was made beautiful simply by being what it is and not pretending to be anything else, just as, perhaps, you can tell whether a politician is being sincere and genuine and not simply mouthing clichés and making promises which have never and can never stand the test of time. Frank knew instinctively what was good, and he was satisfied with no further analysis, for beauty refused to hide round corners and was not afraid to reveal itself to those who had the capacity to behold it. He gave the same seal of validation to Puccini, whose work never failed to bring tears to his eyes. For tears may tell us many different things, but they are also the messengers of beauty. His taste in music, like the best of his memories, was bitter-sweet.

Markus would offer to take Frank out and about in his wheelchair, an offer which Frank accepted from time to time. But it was essential to avoid the site, indeed the vicinity, of The Red Lion. The Red Lion was, of course, no more; neither was the rubble at which Frank had once stood staring. Instead, they had erected a tall red-brick building called The Office of Correction. Every city and town, even very moderately-sized towns, had one of these. They stood ugly against the grey skylines, and presented a depressing aspect when it rained; and it seemed to rain a great deal now, or so Frank thought. Their stated purpose was chiefly to monitor the activities of repeat offenders, those who had committed crimes under the broad heading of ISI. In addition, however, they functioned as a general policing agency, a house of spies intent upon checking any deviation from what was considered to be right and proper conduct. Repeat offenders, now released from their custodial sentences, were required to report weekly or twice-weekly to their local Office of Correction; they were required to submit a report either from their employers or from officially vetted referees, which really amounted to a kind of character-reference, which was then stamped and kept on file; meanwhile, officers would patrol the streets, especially in the dead of night, and woe betide anyone caught taking liberties with the authorities, especially after curfew, which is to say after eleven p.m. in summer, and ten p.m. in winter, for in such cases there would be immediate resort to a custodial sentence, and a very lengthy one for repeat offenders. Alcohol, a strictly forbidden substance, but still available on the black market, was considered to be one of the main attractions for both first-time and repeat offenders alike.

Frank wanted to go nowhere near the Office of Correction. Otherwise memories would flood back, memories too painful to recall; too much had been lost; too much irretrievably gone. But every time Markus wheeled Frank out, Frank felt obliged to give careful directions to places as far distant from the Office of Correction as possible; he could not take the risk that Markus would make a mistake during one of Frank's many naps en route and that he would awaken to find himself face-to-face with that monstrosity of an edifice; it would be a waking nightmare, and one of a kind he could not, at his age, afford to experience.

It was quite inevitable, therefore, that Frank would finally say something about Percy. Just how far young Markus would appreciate the enormity of such matters was uncertain. After all, Markus had practically grown up with the phenomena of ISI and the Office of Correction, and the risk, as Frank saw it, was that Markus would simply take the status quo very much for granted and wonder what all the fuss was about. But then, what did it matter? Frank was too old to care too much. *So what* if Markus greeted everything with 'Yeah' and 'Right!' At least Frank could finally get things off his chest. He therefore determined to say something the next time he and Markus were out together.

This determination brought Percy back firmly and squarely into the frame, giving Frank further cause for reflection during his lonely wheelchair hours. What was it exactly about Percy that had attracted Frank? At first perhaps the loss of their wives, their shared grief and loneliness. Yes, but there was a lot more to it than that. Something in Percy's face, was it? That face with those piercing blue eyes that seemed to see all the way through you, and those thin, sharp features, which, come to think of it, might have made Percy a dead ringer for Sherlock Holmes – at least in the days when they still allowed the original stories and based movies upon them, for they had banned all reference to Sherlock's pipe as soon as the imbibing of tobacco had been made unlawful and replaced the Sherlock that Henry, himself a pipe-smoker, had loved with little more than a cardboard cut-out; and all this unbeknown to Arthur Conan Doyle, who would have scoffed at the prediction that Sherlock's days were to be numbered by ISI.

Was it something in Percy's face that has attracted Frank? Most certainly, there was nothing that could be described as sexual interest or attraction. But surely the face went with what Percy said, and what Percy said emanated from a mind – a mind that was worth knowing, and Frank knew this instinctively, just as he knew the beauty of Bach and Puccini.

Did Frank feel the same towards young Markus? Markus was a mathematician. Percy loved words – at least he spoke a lot and so used a lot of them, but he also spoke *about* them. Words are not the same as mathematics. So Markus and Percy were separated by different spheres of interest. But if Frank was attracted to Percy, and if Markus was attracted to Frank, then maybe Markus would also be attracted to Percy – and this seemed rather logical, and because it was logical it felt also a bit mathematical. Anyway, this bit of nonsense was not altogether nonsensical. Frank decided that he had been attracted to Percy on account of Percy's deep sincerity on matters of truth and man's inhumanity to man – yes, that's right, he remembered now how Percy used to talk about such themes – in fact, it was just this kind of stuff that landed him in trouble with the authorities. There was a kind of beauty in Percy's concern; and Frank knew this instinctively, too.

Thoughts, many of them misgivings, rushed through Frank's poor old head. What would happen if Frank related all this to Markus? What if he told him all about Percy? What if he opened up? Could he trust Markus? Or would Markus just shrug it all off and move on to something completely different? If Markus discounted everything, Frank would feel silly, and also that he had let Percy down in some sort of weird way. It might be like punishing Percy again, even in death. And Percy should never have been punished in the first place. No, he should have been honoured and praised. Percy's big thing had been words: how dangerous they are or might become, but also how beautiful they might be, on the right lips, or from the pens of the good and the wise. Words were powerful, Percy had said. Power is dangerous in the wrong hands, and power can even defile the hands of the righteous; but then, beauty also is powerful, and how wonderful it is to make a legacy of them, as Shakespeare and a thousand poets have done and as many more, not at all so gifted, have done with words of sincerity and love. What was it that John Merrick said in that old movie *The Elephant Man*? Ah, yes, '*I am happy every hour of the day. My life is full, because I know I am loved.*' Such simple words from the deformed mouth of a creature of monstrous aspect immediately stamped him *human*, like a Quality Control label *Passed*.

Oh, dear! Suppose Frank said such things to young Markus? Frank felt hopeless and stupid in turns with such a pattern of thoughts. He finally decided to try the thin end of the wedge, to say something and see what happened. He would not have long to wait. Tomorrow Markus had arranged to take him out and about, just a little amble down one of the leafy roads nearby, leafy because summer had ended, autumn had begun in what promised to be an Indian summer, and the leaves were falling, nature's waste, nature's fallen, were cluttering up the pavements in myriad shades of crumpled brown.

*　　*

'Did I tell you about Percy?'

Frank was wrapped up in a blanket covering his chest and the upper part of his legs; he wore a flat cap and his hands were protected against the cold by a pair of red mittens.

'I said, did I tell you about Percy?' he looked back and up, as best he could at Markus, who wore a green anorak with the hood up. Markus shook his head.

'Anyway ... he was ... Can you stop, Markus. Markus! Stop a minute!'

'You alright?'

'Perfectly. Look, I just want to tell you about my friend Percy.'

'Oh, yeah.'

'Yeah … I mean, yes. Yes, I do. It might be good to know something about him. Anyway, it would explain why I don't want to go anywhere near the House of Correction.'

'Okay!' said Markus, rubbing his hands with the cold and hoping that this wouldn't take very long.

'Well, there's a bench round the corner somewhere here, isn't there? Take me there.'

Markus sat on the bench facing Frank in his wheelchair while Frank told him a little about Percy. He wanted it to be just a little, so he mentioned how he and Percy and Henry used to meet in The Red Lion and what good talks they used to have about this and that and how well-read Percy was and how he used to talk about words and the power of words.

'You see? I mean, I respected him, admired him so much, and, well, then he died, and he left me a note. I have it here, I brought it with me this morning, just to show you.' Frank fumbled a bit under his blanket and produced the envelope.

'Go on, have a look. Be careful with it!'

Markus took the piece of paper out of the envelope, unfolded it carefully, and read it silently.

'No, read it out loud. Read it to me. Go on!'

Markus read the lines:

'*Mary had a little lamb,*

Whose fleece was white as snow,

And everywhere that Mary went

The lamb was sure to go.'

And after the briefest pause said, 'Oh, right,' with an air of nonchalance that seemed to irritate Frank.

'What do you mean, "Oh, right"'? said Frank brusquely.

'I don't know. Maybe your friend, er …'

'Percy.'

'Percy. Yes. Well, maybe he was a bit gone in the head!'

'What!'

'Or maybe it's some kind of conundrum.'

'A what?'

'A conundrum. You know what a conundrum is?'

'Well, I know it isn't a bloody percussion instrument!'

'Right. Well, maybe that's what it is.'

'Take me home, Markus, will you?' Frank sighed. For the time being he had had enough conversation.

'Right,' said Markus.

That was the end of their exchanges that day, the short way home was accomplished without any further attempt at communication, apart from the customary and perfunctory 'Thanks very much' at the end of it, and 'Right, see you next time!' from Markus.

12
Markus Vindicated

As Markus left, closing the door behind him, Frank managed to wheel himself into the living room, close to the window, and looked out onto a mist that had now developed and through which he could make out the shapes of the trees that loomed in the distance, which were beginning to look like ominous shadows; it was altogether a grey, cold and depressing autumnal scene, the kind of scene which had not mattered a jot to a far more youthful Frank, but which was taking its toll now; more so because it mirrored the way Frank was now feeling. As feared, Markus was too young and altogether too flippant to understand the gravity of things, of feelings, of the way Frank felt about Percy; he was incapable of understanding the admiration, the respect, the love that Frank felt for him, and still felt for him, even now. It was obvious – Frank's expectations had been too high. He smiled at his own folly, for what could be expected from a young mathematician, steeped in cold equations and dehumanised rules, when confronted with Mary and her little lamb? And what did mathematicians, more at home with symbols indecipherable to the layman, know or care about *words*? In fact, Markus could be forgiven for thinking that Frank himself was 'a bit gone in the head'. No, Frank had misjudged the whole thing. The hope was that young Markus would have forgotten about it all by the time he came round again; certainly, Frank himself would never bring the subject up again.

* *

It is an enduring, if not always endearing, trait of human nature that the conclusions we arrive at, though mistaken, may appear so solid and unshakeable that any suggestion that we may be in error is shrugged off in contempt.

Imagine, therefore, Frank's surprise when the very next day young Markus unexpectedly rang the doorbell, for nothing had been arranged for another outing; indeed, Frank had entertained the thought that Markus might never again be interested in these perambulations.

'I've been thinking!' said Markus, rushing into the living room like one demented, brushing past Frank and leaving him at the door. Frank wheeled himself into the living room wondering what on earth to expect.

'What your friend …'

'Percy.'

'Yes. The verse he wrote. It was written in 1830, you know, by Sarah Josepha Hale, and there's more!' Markus read from a sheet of paper he took from his pocket:

'He followed her to school one day,
Which was against the rules.
It made the children laugh and play
To see a lamb at school.

And so the teacher turned it out,
But still it lingered near.
He waited patiently about,
'Til Mary did appear.

Why does the lamb love Mary so?
The eager children cried.
Why, Mary loves the lamb, you know,
The teacher did reply.'

Frank just sat there, smiling.

His conclusions had to be reconsidered. Markus had about him the schoolboy enthusiasm that Frank had long ago seen, and somehow loved, in Percy. Suddenly, the autumnal scenes that had so depressed him dissolved into nothing and the prospects seemed brighter. 'Well … well that's amazing … I mean, er yes. Yes, indeed,' is all Frank could come out with, while Markus, bright-eyed and bushy-tailed, seemed poised to deliver some kind of illuminating commentary, as though an ancient scroll had suddenly landed on the living-room carpet from Mount Olympus and was simply begging to receive the merit it had coveted since time immemorial.

'You see, maybe I was right. Maybe it's a kind of conundrum – a puzzle!'

'Well, I don't know …' Frank began, still smiling.

'Unless he'd really lost it – second childhood and all that …'

'No, no. Percy was all there,' said Frank, thoughtfully, and no longer smiling.

'Well, anyway, something to think about,' said Markus, with Frank slowly nodding in absent-minded agreement. 'Well, must be off!' said Markus, as he left with the same gusto as he had arrived, leaving Frank in a state of unsettling wonder. And the subject was dropped.

*   *

Things were not the same after that surprise visit and brief exchange. Over the next few visits, Frank told Markus a lot more about Percy and Henry and their weekly get-togethers in The Red Lion. He actually showed him a photograph of The Red Lion, which assumed a place of honour in the middle of a bookshelf. He told him about Wild Bill and The Yellow Rose of Texas, which had Markus in stitches. But, most of all, he told him about Percy, about Percy's interest in words, his interest in history, and his references to people he and Henry had never heard about before, like George Fox and James Naylor; Markus had never heard of them, either, and seemed to become keenly attentive.

'Sorry for rambling on like this,' said Frank, during one of these little sessions, after they had returned from one of their outdoor excursions.

'Ramble as much as you like, Frank – I'm intrigued.' And he really did sound as though he meant it. 'Hang on, let's make a cuppa, first.' Markus was making himself quite at home in Frank's little place. Frank enjoyed the fact, and he wished he'd had a son like Markus, but that was a fact that he dared not tell him, no, at any rate not yet, no, in no way; but he felt it all the same; and a man can't help what he feels, right or wrong. But you had to be careful with your feelings, especially when they involved relationships; after all, if you get too close, you might live to lose what you're so close to; and Frank had lost Sal, and then the two friends who had helped to keep him going; no, there was a case for keeping one's distance; after so many losses, further losses became unaffordable.

Frank ventured to tell him about Percy's weird theories, and soon got into a muddle.

'Well, it was something about circles or spirals … and er …'

'Sounds like geometry.'

'No, Percy was a history teacher – it was all about history – about things moving in circles … what was the word? Percy was very fond of words, as I told you. Now what *was* the word? You know, as you get older, you forget the little things … But it started with con… cont… contin… uity. That's it! *Continuity*! The continuity of history – as though everything that happens has happened before and er … will happen again. Different horse, same rider, he used to say. Or was it same horse, different rider? Anyway, something like that. Yes, *will happen again* – well, that's the downside. I'm sure Percy depressed himself with such thoughts. Poor old Percy! *Will happen again.*'

'Or, *is* happening right now,' Markus added.

'Yes, right.'

All this stuff about continuity seemed a bit off to Frank, as it had to both he and Henry when Percy first started talking about it – so much so that they were ready to start thinking the worst about Percy's mental state and to explain it away in terms of senility or dementia. But both he and Henry had eventually changed their minds and were ready to believe that there might be something in it after all.

'Yes, and he had this … well, he expressed himself in a strange way, Markus. I remember this … wait a moment, it's all coming back now: *Yesterday, the day before yesterday, and all our yesterdays, are one – and today is tomorrow's yesterday!* Odd, isn't it?' Frank sank back into his armchair with a smile of satisfaction, as though he had achieved a feat of memory to be proud of.

'Fascinating!'

'Really?' said Frank. No doubt Markus was being kind; or, at worst, sarcastic.

What is a meaningless jumble of colours and shapes to one man may represent an incomparable work of art to another, and it may be the devil's job to decide which of them is right; so much so that it may be easier to dismiss both as representing two opposing poles of the same lunatic fringe.

Be that as it may, when Frank related to Markus Percy's so-called theory of historical continuity, it seemed to strike a chord in the mind of young Markus; perhaps it was quite natural that the seed should find a home in the mind of a mathematician.

'No, it's not as daft as it sounds,' explained Markus, with his back to Frank, as he made tea in the kitchen. 'I mean, if the variables are constant, and if you follow the same rules, you get the same result. See?' Markus went on, returning to the living room and placing a cup of tea within Frank's reach

'Hmm,' Frank nodded, with a blank look on his face.

And the subject was dropped, with Frank no wiser, but ever so pleased.

*   *

Between visits, Frank continued to stare out of the window at the changing seasons. The continuity of change was something he could understand, for he saw that with his own eyes, just as night followed day and day followed night; summer, autumn, winter, spring – one followed the other with a kind of ... well, yes, *mathematical* certainty, like numbers in a series. Perhaps Markus ... well, anyway, mathematics wasn't Frank's forte, and he really didn't want to think much more about it. There was, these days, only one kind of continuity that Frank was obliged to contemplate: death followed life, and there was no getting away from that. A man may shed tears for what he has lost; Frank had become capable of shedding them for what he knew was to come; and it would come, as it came for all men, kings and paupers, idiots and the wise, rich and poor. Frank recalled the dictum that a coward dies many deaths and a brave man only one; but he came to know that it is not simply the coward that must face innumerable deaths but also he who is unfortunate enough to reflect beyond the confines of stultifying routine. For the continuity of death is a reflection that tops the most punishing of mortgages, being unrepayable and undeniable. If this is the kind of stuff that went through Percy's head, all Frank could say was 'Poor old chap' – a sentiment that he could now apply to himself. As though it wasn't enough to weep for the tragedies of the past, Percy must have wept for the tragedies to come, to say nothing of those that must be present! It was enough to send an insomniac to sleep, if only to escape from thinking too much. 'Just hope his dreams were sweeter than his waking hours,' Frank muttered to himself.

Frank continued to enjoy Markus's company and looked forward to his visits, for these seemed to lighten Frank's sense of loss. If Frank had believed in reincarnation, and it must be said emphatically that he did not, he might have thought that Percy had been resurrected in the person of Markus. In mathematics Frank was way out of his depth, but Markus was much more interested to talk about history, which only served to heighten Frank's oddball notion that he was talking to a younger version of Percy. If Markus had actually looked like a younger version of Percy, Frank might have felt taken up into some kind of supernatural vortex. Thankfully, Markus's bright blue eyes contrasted with Percy's dark green-brown, and Markus was tall and thin, while Percy was shorter and rather more broad-shouldered; and Frank took further comfort in the fact that Markus sported a short beard while Percy was always clean-shaven and, as far as he could tell, had always been so.

Yes, but, all the same, the similarities were quite striking.

'I think I know where he was coming from,' said Markus, his piercing eyes staring straight ahead, seemingly at nothing in particular. They stopped at the top of a grassy embankment, which led down to the river, while the occasional car sped along the road behind them. Markus put the brake on Frank's wheelchair. 'Quite a view, isn't it?' he remarked. From the embankment you could look down on the rooftops of the northern town below, while the call to prayers rose up from the minarets that stood out quite clearly from the buried landscape.

'Yes. What do mean *coming from*?'

'I've been reading – quite a bit actually. Trying to make up for lost time. We hardly touched it in school …'

'No, well, it's …'

'Anyway,' Markus went on hurriedly, 'seventeenth century. Civil War. Puritanism and all that. Everybody thinking they're right and the other man wrong. And everyone so *certain* about it! Certainty can be a real bugger. Those Puritans – they thought it was all done and dusted. The Roman Catholic Church, once upon a time, was the lifeblood of the country, to have doubted it would have seemed perverse. But then it became anathema, and the Anglican Church replaced it – one corpus of certainty was replaced by another – see? And not without suffering and bloodshed. And then the Anglican Church was rejected, too, again not without suffering and bloodshed … because the Puritans thought their corpus was superior to anything else – they thought this was the best way to ensure right living, the best way to establish order and discipline – the best way to bring everyone else in line with what they thought was God, and if this meant further suffering and bloodshed, well, so be it. And once in power, these Puritans could do what they liked – and what they liked best was to stop everyone else from doing what they liked! Any idea that God was a personal God, any idea that the kingdom of heaven was within you, and not somewhere outside – well, such things were considered blasphemous; in fact, any attempt to let people think for themselves was severely punishable because they thought it licentious; and to question the authority of the Puritans was to preach anarchy – and when I say such things were punishable, I mean punishable by the most cruel torture and … and death … death in ways unimaginable!'

Markus's voice had risen to a crescendo, while Frank stared down at the rich green grass of the embankment and said nothing. Markus paused for breath, but he hadn't finished.

'And all this submission-or-death … just madness, insanity. There are no words to describe it. And that's why the Quakers suffered under the Puritans. But even the Quakers had to have their turn – they, too, degenerated, becoming obsessed about their clothes – so what started as a plea for simple living became an obsession about what they should wear, the colours that were acceptable or unacceptable – even the furniture in their houses became a matter of do-or-die – as though you couldn't expect to get into Heaven unless your face fitted. Strange, isn't it, how religions have progressively less and less to do with Christianity! And as for modern society—'

But Markus stopped abruptly and did not complete his sentence.

'Oh, I'm sorry, Frank! You'll catch a chill. We'd better get home.' Frank nodded, and said nothing. The wind had come up and blew through the grass on the embankment. Suddenly everything seemed to feel unsafe, insecure, if not strangely alien, and Frank longed to sit in his living room embraced by the familiar minutia of his surroundings. But he felt he had not heard the last of Markus's tirade; this was not the end of his dangerous litany, a litany reminiscent of Percy's outburst in The Red Lion; thank God, if there was still a God loving and listening, that Markus's lecture had been delivered on the embankment to an audience of one, and not to a crowd in the market place.

* *

On his next visit, Markus had something revealing to say, though Frank was not at all sure that it was a revelation he wanted to hear. It concerned *Mary had a little lamb*, the nursery rhyme Percy had penned for Frank.

'So there we are,' said Markus, nodding with conviction, and having said that the lamb is the *Spirit*, Mary is the *Messenger* of the Spirit, and the school which turns out the lamb means those who *reject* the Spirit! 'QED! – Yes?'

'Right, well, I suppose you could …'

'Exactly!' said Markus, giving Frank a thumbs-up.

'You're very sure of yourself.'

'But you said Percy was no fool and wasn't demented. So, why not? It's perfectly possible, anyway. It would explain the conundrum. Very neat.'

'If it *was* a conundrum. I mean, many things are possible.'

'Granted. I may be wrong. Very wrong.'

Frank was relieved to hear from Markus's own lips that he might be wrong, more so that he might be *very* wrong. There was something refreshing about that. Something reassuring.

*   *

On another occasion, Markus, inspired by Percy's alleged interest in words, was prompted to mention George Fox's refusal to grant that Scripture was *holy* because writings, consisting of words, cannot be holy but only the *Spirit* that informs them.

'Yes, and then they asked him if the Bible was the Word of God, and he said God was the Word, and the Scriptures were writings, and the Word existed before the writings did, and that the Word fulfilled the writings. And then they asked him if he thought he was a son of God, and he said yes, because he believed that all men and women were the sons and daughters of God. So, you see, he was up before the judges time and again, and time and again they tried to bait him and trap him. Oh, he was clever alright – but that didn't stop them from sending him to prison, and keeping him there under the worst possible conditions. Maybe they were afraid to kill him – but he had to be got rid of, because they couldn't allow anyone to think for himself – he might encourage others to do the same. Ring a bell? People are crucified over and over. And now we've got ISI to guide us and keep us in our places.'

None of this made much sense to Frank – or perhaps he resisted any attempt to make sense of it. It was the last part that particularly worried him and which prompted him to yawn – a sure sign that the old man had had enough.

In his armchair by the window, Frank now had more to think about than he wanted. He began to hope that Markus would soon find a job, a *real* job, a full-time job – a job that would require all of him. That would be good for Markus, and what was good for Markus would also be good for Frank. That is what he told himself, over and over again. Come to think of it, Markus had never mentioned a girl – too busy with his studies, no doubt. It would be good if he found a nice girl. Yes, a nice girl and a nice job. Something safe. Something secure. Something untouchable, at least untouchable in a way that people like George Fox, and, for that matter, Percy, were not. Frank wanted to think smooth, unbarbed, unjagged, distinctly safe thoughts, thoughts about which one could be certain, without getting oneself and others into trouble, because Markus was at least right about one thing – certainty could be a bugger.

Frank had always remembered that line from his schoolboy Shakespeare – somewhere in *King Lear* – 'Bear free and patient thoughts'. It would be nice if one were able to bear free and patient thoughts one's whole life through. But whether or not Markus's thoughts, like Percy's, were dangerous, Frank could not help but admire his enthusiasm – almost like a virgin astonishment at the wrongs of the world and the strongest desire to right them. But, of course, one could not right the sins of the past. If only Time could be reasoned with, if only it were possible to right the sins of the past! But Time could not be reasoned with; no, it marched on regardless, not giving a fig for the consciences of good men or the pain they suffer for what they have lost – all of us putty in the hands of Time, even if the sins we committed were all down to us.

No, the kind of advice Frank had eventually decided to offer Markus was to play things down and play things safe. For he had convinced himself that there was the best case imaginable for playing things safe. He remembered how the tears had filled Sal's eyes when news arrived of her father's death. He had held her close and comforted her with the words, 'We shall always be together.' But death and disease have other ideas. And he could never accept that she had gone and that he remained. Death and disease taught hard lessons, and we had to be wise enough to learn them – you had to hold on to life, your own and that of those you loved. Human beings might be notoriously bad students, but somehow you had to hold on to your priorities with a steel-like grip despite yourself. Would not a good father give such advice to his only son? And such advice was especially valid in those dangerous times, although Frank was hard put to think of a time that was not dangerous, because it was all down to what human beings were capable of – of some great good, but of much unspeakable harm.

All of which might seem reasonable enough. So reasonable, indeed, that it is not immediately clear why the conversation between them took the turn it did when the next opportunity presented itself to warn Markus of dangerous waters and to advise him to hug the shoreline.

13

Happy Ever After?

Autumn had advanced, and the grass on their favourite spot on the embankment was frosted over and crunched underfoot. Frank was well-blanketed and wore mittens and a woolly bobble hat, and Markus was blatantly hatless, a sure sign that the generation gap was alive and well. It was no place to linger long.

Markus was about to embark on one of his tirades, this time inspired by his reading of a short article claiming that dissident poetry had been discovered in the archives of the local library. Dissident poetry, or dissident writing of any sort, was of course defined and outlawed as such by ISI, and those found in possession of it, let alone disseminating it, were subject to the most rigorous interrogation, so rigorous indeed that it was all too often considered preferable to own up and face the music, which almost invariably meant a spell in a Rehabilitation Centre. News of the discovery had been published in a weekly broadsheet, for the authorities wished to make as much as possible out of it for its propaganda value to further its latest *Let Us Root Out Troublemakers* campaign; these campaigns were mounted every so often, even if the events that inspired them were more alleged than real, or even if they were completely fabricated. Freedom of expression, like freedom of the press, was of course a thing of the past, and anything submitted for publication, in whatever format, had to be vetted by the Board of Censors, and woe betide any author who was deemed a threat to social cohesion. Any reference, for example, to sexual acts or relations between men and women needed to be veiled in such a way as to avoid the long and twisted arm of the law, a requirement that was mirrored also in filmmaking; love scenes were a thing of the past, in particular any scene in which either party felt the need to disrobe. The same had long applied to physical depictions of homosexual relations; and, more recently, even mere references to homosexual relations, physical or otherwise, were coming under the scrutiny of the ISI, and the banning of such references was discussed very favourably in the regular broadsheets, a sure sign of what was to follow, for what was discussed favourably in the broadsheets was very much on the cards – indeed, merely by reading the brief 'discussions' in the broadsheet one could predict with near-certainty the course of the law.

Frank interrupted Markus before the latter could get into his stride, astonishing himself in the process.

'Can you write?'

'What?'

'Write! You know, put pen to paper – make sentences …'

'I suppose.'

'Well, then. Do that. Write it all down. What you're saying. Write it down. On paper. Pen and ink. Don't use your computer. And let's get out of here. I'm freezing to death!'

Markus slowly moved Frank away from the embankment.

'I'd never get it published!'

'Of course not. Do it, anyway. It's a good therapy. Buy a good, a *very* good, notebook. *Very* good pen and ink – and write, and write, and write 'til you've got nothing left to say – and that'll take quite a while I should imagine. And, who knows? One day it might turn up somewhere – you know, like things in a time capsule – and somebody might read it – maybe people better than the lot of us – and then they'd know that we weren't all cretinous ruffians – they'd know some us had some sense of decency.'

'What would I write in this very good notebook?' Markus asked with a smile.

'Oh, for God's sake! Write what you're telling me and all you *want* to tell me. Oh, and do it for me, and for Percy! You can use me as a sounding board, if you like. Oh, yes. I'd have a few things to say before my time's up.'

'You sound very bitter.'

'Yes, just like you, you mean? Bitter? Yes, well maybe "contemptuous" is a better word – must be careful with our words, you know.

'Percy once said he'd like a penny for every word he wiped off the whiteboard – he'd have been a rich man. Anyway, yes, contemptuous – anyone who values goodness can't help being contemptuous about man's inhumanity to man – and that's what worries you, isn't it. Anyway, as I said, write it all down. That's all we've got in the end – words. Just words. Better than nothing.'

'You don't sound very hopeful.'

'Aah! Well, I'm an old man. Look at me! My business is the business of old men – to warn. I'll leave hope to you. Come on! Let's get out of here!'

Markus did not know quite how to take this outburst. He had never heard Frank speak like that before. In turns he thought of him as a harbinger of doom and as an ancient sage who had seen the beginning of the world and regretted its subsequent development.

As for Frank, he was as puzzled as Markus. What had happened to all those thoughts about playing it down and playing it safe? On the contrary, he was encouraging Markus to be as seditious as he liked and, in doing so, caution was thrown to the wind. It was clearly time for second thoughts: Sal had died, and Frank was on his own, and soon he too would be gone and forgotten. There were limits to how far you felt you had to play it safe – because there were also things you had to do, and to say and, above all, to be; to do, say and be before your time was up. While you lived you were a friend, a husband, a father –

but, then, you were also more than all three, and you had to be true to whatever that *more* was. There was something precious and inviolate deep inside that made a man a *good* friend, a *good* husband, a *good* father, and if it was not there, nothing could put it there; and it was something that could not be forever ignored, forever subdued, forever subservient to tyrants, nor yet mediocrity; it was like a wild beast with good intentions which, once released, might admittedly pave the way to Hell but which had to be given its full rein.

It was as though Percy himself had returned, speaking through Frank as a ventriloquist speaks through his doll. Some doll! Wheelchair-bound, with nowhere to go but to the window in the living room of his small apartment.

*   *

Markus had obviously taken things to heart. He bought himself an excellent notebook, with a blue cover and with pages lined and smooth as silk, and a pen with a gold nib, and ink aplenty.

And he started to write; and he wrote and he wrote; and each time he finished writing he would carefully place notebook, pen and ink in a drawer of his desk, a drawer which he would unfailingly lock; and he kept the key, not on his keyring, but behind one of the books on his bookshelf that happened to be written by his namesake – the *Meditations* of the Roman emperor Markus Aurelius Antoninus Augustus. The irony of this hiding place was not lost on Markus, for he learned that Aurelius had been most grateful to his teacher and mentor, Alexander of Cotiaeum, for the emphasis he had placed on the meticulous use of words and on the development of impeccable literary style, and, if this was not sufficiently ironic, given Frank's account of Percy's emphasis on the importance of words, he also came to learn that the persecution of Christians increased markedly during this Roman's period of office, despite the fact that Aurelius was the last of the so-called Five Good Emperors; which seemed to suggest, therefore, that whatever wisdom was contained within the pages of the *Meditations* and however keen its author was to leave to posterity a shining example of literary accomplishment and philosophical sagacity, a reflective mind was consistent with unspeakable cruelties; it seemed to show the enormous lengths to which men would go, or the limitless depths to which they would descend, to preserve social cohesion and political stability. Markus was fascinated by his namesake and repeatedly read his *Meditations* from cover to cover in a vain effort to exonerate him; vain, that is, except to grant that Aurelius had been a victim of his time; but then, since we are all victims of our time, Markus was reluctant to let him off the hook; Aurelius was in the dock, and would never leave it. Moreover, the first two centuries Anno Domini were uncomfortably beginning to resemble the present. What was it, again? *Yesterday, the day before yesterday, and all our yesterdays, are one – and today is tomorrow's yesterday.*

* *

Markus was a mathematician through and through, yet his bookshelves creaked with his burgeoning collection of history books. No less so when he finally landed a junior lectureship and felt the pain of having to move furniture and books to a new apartment, in a new location nearer to his place of work. He said his goodbyes to Frank, promising to visit him during vacations, and Frank had wished him all the best.

'A new adventure!' Frank said, with a faint smile on his lips. 'And don't forget the notebook!' he added.

'What? – oh yes. Right.'

Frank had got his wish – Markus had a nice job, teaching mathematics to first-year undergraduates. New adventures invariably require new relationships, but these would inevitably follow once Markus had found his feet, or in the very process of finding them, and with such thoughts Frank contented himself, giving himself the customary fatherly reassurances.

College 'societies', which had once abounded, and to which both students and teaching staff were welcomed in the advertising literature, had dwindled to single figures. The Christian Society had all but fizzled out, its place taken by the Islamic Society, membership of which was extended to all and sundry in the hope of making ever larger numbers of converts, a hope that was proving well-founded.

The History Society, to which Markus was particularly drawn, was very much in decline, partly because its programme was so predictable; members met in order to listen to scripted talks on the importance of the preservation of social order throughout history, as though every war fought and every campaign, military or otherwise, ever conducted was done so in the interests of *social cohesion*, which had become a catchphrase; lack of social cohesion covered a multitude of sins, while its establishment was the universal balm and panacea towards which the whole human race had, consciously or unconsciously, directly or indirectly, been aiming. Social cohesion was the new framework in which history itself was to be understood, as though prior to this astonishing insight events had lacked a *grammar* which could sensibly express the teleology of history; because, it was perceived, history must have a point, a horizon towards which everything groped. Anything or anyone, therefore, who appeared to question the grammar of history obviously misunderstood what history was all about; but nobody did question the grammar – at least, not until Markus dared to ask questions.

And to those who might possibly doubt whether all history might be explained in terms of social cohesion, or whether the phrase itself was immediately clear, the usual rejoinder was that there was every reason to support efforts to simplify matters; simplification was tantamount to cutting the Gordian Knot of historical events, allowing a welcome degree of illumination into the otherwise impenetrable forests of darkness that invariably characterised conflicting interpretations of the very same events. Which is why Markus … but our narrative moves too fast.

Markus had already met Simon, a lanky historian in his mid- to late forties, good-looking, certainly, and with a good head of hair which had turned prematurely white; they had met in one of the college's recess rooms on Markus's very first evening. The occasion was the customary Interdepartmental Induction Evening (IIE), held at the very start of the academic year and designed to allow new recruits to meet existing incumbents. It must be said that recess rooms were the non-alcoholic equivalent of college bars; but the word 'bar' was in the process of being expunged from the language, as was alcohol from the routine intake of all college employees. The general social consensus these days was that bars had been no better than 'dens of iniquity'. So, in the recess rooms, coffee, tea, fruit juices and strictly non-alcoholic beers were all the beverages available, alcohol being reserved for the black market which, unsurprisingly, was doing a rip-roaring trade. Recess rooms were almost invariably half-empty, except on Induction Evenings, when an air of enthusiasm amongst new arrivals and a natural though temporary curiosity amongst older hands would whip up trade for an hour or so.

Simon, eyeing Markus from the other side of the room, had taken the initiative and elbowed his way across the floor with arm extended.

'What? Markus? Mathematics? Not my forte, I'm afraid,' Simon said briskly and loudly, over the hum of conversation. 'Me? History. Yes, the History Faculty.'

Which was music to Markus's ears. He considered himself off to a very good start; which was far better than he had expected after meeting his own colleagues, notably Alfredo, who immediately began a litany of complaints over his own teaching schedule which, he claimed, had been put together by a family of chimpanzees, and Samantha ('Call me Sam – everybody does'), a youngish woman, pale, if not anaemic, and thin as a pencil, who stuck around long enough to shake hands and then seemed to scamper off into another corner of the bar, quite oblivious to the customary offices of polite talk and intrapersonal inquiry. 'Oh, that's Sam – take no notice of her!' said Alfredo, quite gratuitously.

But it was refreshing, not to say exciting, to meet Simon. He was different, if only for being a historian.

'Oh, Markus – meet Rash,' said Simon, looking quickly from one to the other.

'Rash?'

'Rashid, actually.'

'Islamic Studies,' said Simon.

'Oh, really!' Markus returned, in a tone undeserving of an exclamation mark. 'Just started?'

'Oh, no! Been quite a few years now.'

Rash then delivered a barrage of questions, including the customary questions about whether Markus was married, or had an intended, or a girlfriend, and what he thought about the place so far; where he was born, what school he had attended, exactly where he lived now, whether he was happy about his flat, whether his accommodation had been arranged by the university, and so on, and all this was interspersed with offers to show Markus round properly, to help him get to know the ropes, and with assurances of help should he ever need to know anything. Rash seemed too good to be true, delivering his solicitations with an air which seemed to mix genuine concern with obeisance, not to say subservience. But then, the occasion seemed to lend itself to a certain degree of exuberance, so that Rash's manner did not seem to justify too much critical scrutiny. It just went to show how high one might get without the help of alcohol or any other form of drug-induced relaxant; the thought flashed through Markus's mind, not remaining long enough to be entertained.

Eventually Rashid moved away, perhaps to interrogate another new face, and Markus and Simon found themselves alone.

'Can't hear you very well – sorry!' said Simon. 'Over there – quiet corner – let's grab it while we've got the chance.'

They moved to the quiet corner and, away from the madding crowd, where the hum of conversation seemed to have been magically reduced, they sat with what was left of their fruit juices.

'So, you told Rash you're not tied down – I mean, no girlfriend, partner?'

'That's right – and you?'

'Nope. Not for me.'

And after a moment's silence the invitation came, as though fate had ordained it long ago.

'Yes, well, feel free to come along. The society welcomes newcomers – anyone interested in history. I don't go so often myself these days, but, anyway, I'll go with you this time. Never know, might be inspiring.'

Yes, it was yet more music to Markus's ears. Here was a historian inviting him to a meeting of the History Society. What would Frank say? Something about Fate? Perhaps Destiny would be a better, more hopeful, word. And who would want to miss an opportunity to be inspired?

'Strange, though,' Simon remarked. 'You're the first mathematician I've met interested in history – I mean, *that* interested. No offence.'

'None taken. I haven't met a historian *that* interested in mathematics, either!'

'Which includes yours truly, I'm afraid.'

They laughed at the joke. It was not much of a joke. The laughter must have been about something else. Their eyes met, and quickly disengaged.

14

A Loose Cannon

The next meeting of the History Society was posted for the following Friday evening, on the eve of Markus's birthday; and what better way to celebrate his birthday than an inspiring lecture given by an inspired speaker. Unfortunately, no speaker had been arranged; instead, it was to be an evening of group discussion, in which someone would begin with a statement and others would be expected to pick it up and run with it; not a bad way to do history, Markus decided, after getting over his initial disappointment. It was arranged for he and Simon to meet up and trot off to the meeting together; however things turned out, it would be fun going with Simon – a newly-found friend to whom he was fondly attracted and very much wanted to like.

'Well, as I see it, it's a bit like Newton's Laws of Motion, or Einstein's Relativity Theory. I mean, to be able to cut through all the hash and look at things afresh. A stroke of genius! You can look at every event, every movement, every historical tendency and explain it perfectly well in terms of social cohesion. That's what we historians are all about these days – and it's a gigantic step forward, and I for one am proud to be a part of it.'

These magnanimous, not to say inspiring, words were spoken by Paul, a corpulent fellow in his mid-fifties, with receding and thinning hair and a moustache that ought to have been trimmed but was overhanging his upper lip and threatened to go ever further into regions hitherto unexplored.

There was a general consensual hum from the group of eight, which was formed in a circle, with Simon and Markus sitting on opposite points of its diameter and therefore facing one another. Simon simply nodded through Paul's preamble.

'I must take issue with all that.' The hum faded out reluctantly, and Simon's nod came to a slow stop, as though he believed himself to have misheard what had just been said. Simon stared unbelievingly across the diameter at what he thought must be a mistaken piece of geometry.

'No, I'm sorry. I just don't understand. I mean, all this stuff about social cohesion just doesn't cut any ice with me.'

'Markus is a mathematician,' Simon put in blandly, as if to pour oil on troubled waters.

'What's that got to do with anything? I'm allowed to think for myself.'

'Of course you are,' said Paul from under his moustache, 'as long as you think correctly. I mean, as a mathematician, you must accept that. Well, it's just the same with history. There are rules, and they need to be followed – otherwise your conclusions will be flawed. I mean to say …' He looked around at the group, smiling as he did so, as if he were appealing to the blatantly obvious.

'Take an example,' said Markus.

'By all means!' said Paul, still smiling round at the others.

'Well, it seems to me like a case of one man's meat is another man's poison. Custer was defeated at the Battle of the Little Bighorn, right? Now, was that in the cause of social cohesion? But just *whose* social cohesion are we talking about? The white man's or the red man's? If it was the white man's social cohesion, it was achieved at the expense of the red man's, and who is to say which social cohesion was right? Even Custer said that had he been born a native American, he would have fought against the white man's incursions.'

'Yes, but …' Paul's moustache twitched noticeably, but its possessor failed to get a word in edgeways.

'Or another example – the holocaust was no doubt seen by the Nazis to be in the interests of social cohesion. It certainly wasn't in the interests of Jewish social cohesion, or anybody else's, and that's why it had to be stopped, and at all costs. Don't you agree?' Markus continued without having received any kind of consensus. 'Or again, Socrates was put on trial because he was considered a troublemaker, but if a man like him is sacrificed on the altar of social cohesion, we are entitled to ask what it's worth, don't you think? No, no, I'm just baffled. I don't see how it helps to talk in terms of social cohesion – it's a hollow phrase, a non-starter – not at all like Newton's and Einstein's contribution to physics, and I'm afraid you just belittle them by comparing their achievements to what you call social cohesion.'

Markus certainly sensed that he had said too much, and perhaps too much for his own good. But he couldn't help himself. After an embarrassing pause that seemed to him, and to Simon, to last a lifetime, Paul piped up in a jovial spirit:

'Ah! A new kid on the block! That's what it is! Now, er "Markus", isn't it? You see, a little knowledge is a dangerous thing. What I think is missing is the bigger picture. Yes, that's it, you're missing the bigger picture – no, please don't be offended. You've made some interesting points, yes, *very* interesting – I think we all agree?' Paul looked round to a pool of nods and grunts. 'Yes, and, may I say, very eloquently put, too. But, and I say this advisedly and with stacks of goodwill, as your knowledge of history widens and deepens, you will, I am sure, come to see the bigger picture. My advice is, *patience*. Patience young man!' Paul's moustache had had its moment of glory at last, and Paul ended his brief peroration by aiming it round the group, with a smile underneath and struggling to be noticed.

Paul, who had obviously established himself as the chairman and driving force of the group, suggested some refreshments before moving on – presumably to consider the bigger picture. Markus made some excuse about having to be somewhere else, and Simon promised to call in and see him later if that were convenient. He was reassured that it would be convenient.

* *

So ended Markus's first, and, as it was to prove, last attendance at the History Society. He went home and headed straight for Aurelius' *Meditations*. It was not very late when Simon knocked the door; he knocked when Markus was about to put the finishing touches to his notebook entry for the day, an entry which concluded: '*So – witnessed the death of history – now a pale and shrivelled corpse. Ludicrous reaction to reason and common sense. Still can't believe it.*' He opened the door to let Simon in, immediately proceeding to replace his notebook, pen and ink in the drawer of his desk.

'What, still working?' Simon entered with a bulging briefcase.

'Not really. What's that?'

Simon produced a bottle of Scotch from his briefcase and a packet of cigarettes.

'Wow!' Markus could hardly believe his eyes.

'Smoke?'

Markus shook his head.

'Do you mind if ...?

Markus shook his head again.

'You won't say no to a stiff one, will you? Get a couple of glasses, then.'

'Taking a bit of a risk, aren't you?' Markus looked unsettled.

'Don't worry – I'll take everything back with me – dump it on the way. You see, it'd be a bigger risk if I invited you over to my place – I mean, being a college residence it's much more closely watched. In fact, they're in the process of installing CCTV all over the place – but we're okay here in your little place, at least for the time being. I mean if you don't mind …'

Markus shook his head. 'Let's live dangerously.' And he watched as Simon carefully poured the precious liquid equally into both glasses and in small measures – glasses intended for long drinks and whose palates were now tested to the full.

'Well, that was a rum business – excuse the pun,' said Simon, as they both settled back into deep armchairs.

'Oh, you mean the so-called History Society?'

'Only so-called?'

'Well …'

Markus was unsure whether to continue in this vein or whether it would be advisable to change the subject; he also wondered whether he should really care either way. He needn't have worried. The evening wore on as they sipped their Scotches and exchanged anecdotes from past and present, and the music from Markus's music deck that nonchalantly, and ever so gently, filled the background became increasingly more noticeable as the Scotch kicked in, seeming to make conversation much less obligatory. A calm and calming atmosphere prevailed, as though whatever should come next need not be resisted, but simply be taken in one's stride. 'Puccini. Just my cup of tea, too,' Simon mumbled, as their eyes met across the short space between their armchairs.

They were half asleep when Simon managed to shake himself fully awake. 'Well, must be off. Good God, I almost forgot! It's your birthday tomorrow, isn't it? Ah, stupid of me!'

'You didn't get that from me!'

'Yes, I did – you mentioned it yourself.'

'Anyway, you've given me a nice birthday present – the Scotch – your company – and so …'

They stood in the doorway while Simon fiddled with the empty bottle of Scotch and his briefcase.

Where the words that followed came from Markus could not tell, but they filled the spaces between these two men and seemed, however improbably, to come from his own lips. But the simplicity of words can nevertheless be momentous. 'You don't have to leave, you know.' These simple words changed the relationship between them forever. And that change received its irreversible stamp of approval when, in the next instant, their eyes met.

* *

What Frank would have made of it all is anybody's guess, or, for that matter, Percy. Percy might have read up on Quakers, but he was far from being one of them; that degree and that kind of moral rectitude was not for Frank – or Percy, and certainly not for poor old Henry. But what they would have made of the scene in Markus's room during that night is quite another matter – 'Well, everyone to his own' is probably the very best reaction that could possibly be expected from any of the three friends.

For all that, these three would have looked at each other with a nod and a benign smile at the words which, as though from thin air, rolled out from Markus's lips that morning as Markus and Simon lay together in Markus's bed as in a vessel becalmed. As they lay on their backs, staring up at the ceiling, the silence broken only by the trills of small birds playing on window sills, Markus said, '*Yesterday, the day before yesterday, and all our yesterdays, are one – and today is* tomorrow's *yesterday.*'

'What? What on earth is that?' mumbled Simon, as though waking up from one dream to the meaningless jumble of another.

'The mantra of the wise. Nothing, really.' Simon responded by snoring lightly, waking a short time later to find Markus dressed and preparing coffee and toast.

'Don't you want to ask what's going on, Simon? Sugar?' Markus had just poured a coffee.

'What? Er, no sugar – just a little milk, please. How d'you mean, *going on*?'

'Well, everything round us. Where shall I start? Having to sneak about with a drop of booze as though a drink or two was an act of sedition. Can't smoke. CCTV cameras installed. Not to mention yesterday's news – you heard? Some yobs smashed up that statue of Quentin Crisp. No? Oh, yes. The one in Chelsea – and it was reported in such a matter-of-fact way, as though it was a weather report – not an iota of protest. It's the same with Jewish cemeteries – desecrated all over the place, and the only ones complaining are the Jews! Who's next? Christians? And I bet there'll be precious little outcry there, too, even from Christians.'

'Yes, well, there's been a spate of monument-bashing recently. Emily Pankhurst took a beating last month and—'

'Yes, and there's no sign of a replacement, either. That's what happens to some things – once down, they're down for good! Don't you find it worrying?' Markus said, giving Simon an inquisitive stare.

'Maybe it's a kind of fad – you know, like a wave that sort of hits the beach, crumples a few sandcastles and then recedes again.'

'Unless it's a tsunami and takes with it what can never be replaced.'

'A bit early for me, I'm afraid, all this stuff. I've got a terrible head – any coffee left?'

But Marcus came to learn that it was not simply too early in the morning for Simon to be overly worried about socio-political tsunamis.

For, subsequently, each time the same theme was approached, Simon would find some way of defusing Markus's enthusiasm, some way of deflecting the arrows loosed from Markus's bow, some way of mitigating criticism, some way of changing the subject and ending in some harmless banter. Finally, Markus gave up trying to encourage Simon to question matters – but not before giving Simon something to think about at his own leisure. It was when Markus was in a particularly awkward frame of mind.

'I think appeasement is at the bottom of it. There's a general tendency towards appeasement, and at the root of appeasement is fear.'

'Here we go!' Simon muttered.

'No, listen! Appeasement has become a kind of obsession, and its strangling us all – suffocating us – turning our democracy into a kind of consortium of appeasers. Dark forces, Simon – dark forces are at work. You must know what's happening. It's no good just burying our heads in the sand, because we might lose what we value most – we should be very worried about that – because if we lose what we value most we might never get it back.'

'What on earth are you talking about, Markus?'

'Lots of things. I'm talking about lots of things. But you're included! You and me!'

'What?'

'Our relationship is fast becoming a criminal offence – AGAIN! – having been decriminalised a long time ago – in the 1960s, for God's sake!'

'It's not exactly a foregone conclusion.'

'Oh, yes, it is. You know it is. You're in denial! Don't you want to ask yourself how that could possibly have happened? And what we can do, what we *have* to do, to stop it happening again? Up to now, nobody seems to be asking these questions. And when you stop asking questions, history repeats itself! Appeasement and fear are at the root of it all. Don't you see? And all because we're trying to accommodate ourselves to an alien set of values, values contrary to our own, and they're turning back the pages of history, so all we've achieved and all we have still to achieve will be less than worthless, because they'll be considered *socially incohesive*. Everything's going backwards, and nobody seems to notice. See?'

'Yes. Yes, alright. And I also see I'm late for my lecture! Pick this up later.'

Simon sped away as good-naturedly as he could manage. But he was put out by this latest harangue, and he did not want to pick it up later. Markus was really a mathematician, and he was nobody's fool, either. But he should really give all this other stuff a rest and just concentrate on what he does best. Yes, no doubt about it. Simon was put out. In particular, the phrase 'You're in denial' stuck fast, burr-like, and would not be shaken off. After all, people in denial may well be validating their own decline, if not demise. Markus was like a nagging wife, and there was just so much of this sort of thing you could reasonably be expected to take.

The fact is, Simon was fast reaching the conclusion that their relationship had staled. That first night in Markus's room had been the best; and since then, things had gone steadily downhill; after all, when passion is spent, you're left with what remains, and if what remains fails to hold you, it seems time to move on. Added to which, Markus, from the word go, and now increasingly so, was sailing his little boat too close to the wind. Simon had been able to put up with it while passion reigned, but if this was to be the way things had to go, the prospects for Markus's future seemed bleak indeed. And talking of futures, it was only reasonable to look to his own.

As for Markus, his increasing frustration with what appeared to be Simon's indifference to questions of enormous importance was leading him even faster and even closer to pastures new. Simon claimed to be a historian, but he appeared to be abdicating his responsibilities, and to such a degree and to such a depth that Markus was finding increasingly deplorable.

Though still on speaking terms, relations cooled between Markus and Simon. Being in love, if that is what it was, had not given way to love, but only to a friendly civility. Passion has a short fuse and a life of passion is not appreciably longer than the fuse that ignites it. Therefore, no more was to be expected than a calm indifference to what had passed before. Week followed week with no very meaningful communication between them. Needless to say, Simon was successful in avoiding the issue which had served to cool their relations or had at least been the occasion of its marked drop in temperature; the subject was never again picked up.

At least, it was not picked up by either Markus or Simon; but neither would it rest like a sleeping dog.

15
Enter Rashid

It was fast approaching Winter Recess, formerly known as the Christmas Vacation, and the wintry sun glinted on the minarets from which the muezzin called the godly to prayer; those minarets, vaguely menacing though yet still somewhat eccentric, which overlooked Barlow Street, on the corner of which once stood a fish and chip shop much patronised by the local populace. Those lofty spiritual edifices stood taller than even Academy House, an office block which had as much connection with Plato's Academy as the moon has with a wedge of cheddar cheese.

When the sunlight gave way to the dark, chill evening air, Simon heard an abrupt knock on his door; opening it, he found Rashid standing in the doorway, smiling, and asking, in his customary and desperately polite manner, if he could possibly intrude. Simon and Rashid could never be described as friends; and to call them acquaintances still fails to hit the mark adequately. For the point is, Rashid was not someone you dared to ignore. As he entered the room, he gave quick looks, right and left, as if he expected to find someone there.

'No, I thought I might be intruding,' he said.

'Not at all.'

'Yes, well, I thought I'd better clear up a few things – er, for the RP, I mean – just routine, you see.'

It needs to be explained that Rashid was a Watcher, and was known by all and sundry to be a Watcher. In fact, Rashid himself would openly joke about it, using the Arabic word 'Murakeb' ('watcher'). His task was to be the eyes and ears of SAC (Supervisory and Advisory Committee) which, in turn, would report to the RP (Review Panel), and it was the Review Panel that would, in the light of the findings of SAC, decide whether or not to extend, or terminate, the contracts of the teaching staff. By joking about his function, Rashid might have been understood to be either faintly ashamed or somewhat incompetent; he was neither; his light-hearted approach was part of a process of ingratiation, winning either the pity or the underestimation of those he watched, while the watched might sometimes wonder whether he was, by force of circumstance or under heinous threat, actually playing a role he despised – such uncertainties were all the better for one who was paid to be the eyes and ears of SAC.

'Clear up?'

'Er, yes. You know how it is – the customary loose ends.' And, while Simon was struggling to work out how it was, Rashid popped the question:

'How is your friend Markus getting on?'

'Markus?' Why should he ask about Markus? What kind of loose end was Markus?

'Well, alright, I suppose. I haven't seen him recently – I mean, not to …'

'Point is, you used to see a lot of each other, didn't you?' Rashid was standing by the window and peering out of it, as though he was trying to catch a glimpse of something outside.

'Much more so than now, yes.'

'Word has it – you will excuse me – word has it that your relationship was quite intimate. Any truth in it?'

There was a time when such a question would have been quite out of order, when Rashid might have been told quite candidly to mind his own business. But then, at such a time as that, Rashid himself would have had the decency to say nothing at all, even if such thoughts had occurred to him, and they might not have occurred to him at all.

But times were very different now; so much so that such matters were of fundamental interest to SAC and carried weight with the Review Panel. Relationships between the teaching staff were frowned upon, and homosexual relations were strictly taboo; the discovery of a homosexual liaison was enough to justify dismissal in as much time as it took to prepare the paperwork and give it the official stamp, and then the prospects of employment elsewhere were subsequently grim, if not out of the question; and there was no indication at all that such strictures may become more relaxed in future; on the contrary, the future looked grimmer than the present. Added to which, no hearing and no defence was possible in such cases; a strong suspicion was sufficient to set the wheels in motion and ensure dismissal.

'I can assure you, there was nothing …' Simon was a model of self-control and spoke slowly and quietly.

'Well, look, I'm not here to judge. In any case, it does not matter too much.' Rashid, no longer grinning, had moved away from the window and was slowly walking round the room, hands clasped behind his back, in a kind of meditative, professorial manner and as though he was almost thinking out loud.

'Well, when I say it does not matter, of course it matters – if true. I mean, *if* it were true, though you say it is *not*, it would matter – yes, it would matter a very great deal. You say it is not true, and that's good enough. Yes. But, even so, it would be better to keep your distance from the subject – I mean, from Markus. Would you mind if we sat down?'

They sat facing each other in deep armchairs. Rashid, resting his elbows on the arms, tapped his hands together as though he were forming the arch of a church.

'You see, this matter, I mean the matter you say is not true, can be waived aside – yes, waived aside completely, and forgotten. The thing is, there is another matter even more disturbing than this matter you say is not true, and it concerns Markus – I mean, Markus directly – not you. Some students have, shall we say, expressed their concern. Er, do you know about this?'

'No, I ...'

'You were nodding.'

'No, I didn't mean ...'

'Alright, no matter ... Yes, they have expressed their concern that some of Markus's lectures are, shall we say, unconventional and, I may say, quite irrelevant. Not only irrelevant, but upsetting no, that's not the word – unsettling, yes, that's it, unsettling.'

'I really know nothing at all ...'

'Right, I thought you didn't. But, on the other hand, were you ever to hear Markus say anything, er, unsettling, you would let me know, wouldn't you? For the sake of the students – for the sake of the university.'

Simon opened his mouth to say he was not sure what, when Rashid interrupted.

'Anyway, I've taken up enough of your time. Must be off,' he said, getting up and moving towards the door.

'You know,' Rashid went on as he stood in the doorway, 'it's refreshing, no, *reassuring* I meant to say, to know people like yourself. I mean, people who love what they do, love their jobs – people who have many years ahead of them doing what they do best.'

With that, he turned and walked away briskly – leaving Simon ill at ease, yet thanking his lucky stars that his relationship with Markus had ended when it did, for it just went to show that in a place like that there was no such thing as covering your tracks, no such thing as keeping things completely under wraps – it was enough to make a man heterosexual, or what they were now increasingly at pains to call 'normal'.

Simon was happy not to have substantiated the innuendoes ever so lightly veiled in the word 'unsettling'. He knew what Rashid was talking about – or at least he thought he did. Markus was, he knew, disgruntled. Simon could never forget those harangues, and the discernible contempt Markus had for him as a historian, a contempt never voiced in strong terms, but, yes, discernible nevertheless. He had known it all along, ever since that time in the History Society. Markus was on a downward path. Simon was too good a man to wish Markus any ill, nor would he willingly incriminate him further; no, he was too good a man for that; but he was not good enough to warn him, either, to or continue to befriend him – no, not now, not under these circumstances; better by far to keep his distance, and perhaps to hope that Markus would not dig a hole for himself deeper than it already was. Accusations of ISI had developed into a nightmare-in-waiting. If Rashid's object had been to isolate Markus by providing a strong disincentive for Simon to continue, let alone deepen, his relationship with the 'subject', his efforts were by no means in vain.

As for the complaints from students to which Rashid had alluded, these consisted in a revealing tête-à-tête with only one student, one to whom Rashid had formed an attachment – an attachment, moreover, which Rashid wished to be rather more than Platonic, and promised to become so with a little more effort and gentle blandishment from Rashid himself. As for the risks attendant on the pursuit of his passions, Rashid considered it far less likely that he himself would become an object of suspicion, since it was not customary to place trusted agents of SAC under surveillance for trespassing upon the rules that they themselves were paid so zealously to uphold and protect. As long as Rashid continued to do a good job catching others out, there was less likelihood of his being caught out himself; and with this simple though not altogether reliable train of thought, Rashid consoled himself, and followed his passions with a reasoned and cautious degree of impunity.

According to the student in question, Markus was apt to deliver some biting asides during what was otherwise a mechanical lesson on some aspect of pure mathematics. Markus was at least careful to make his asides during a natural break in one of his lectures, or perhaps near the end, and might begin with some such phrase as 'By the way, have you ever thought …?' The aside might consist of something political, but more often historical – for on the question of historical development he appeared to be rather fixated. He was apt to compare the development of history with equations in mathematics. On one occasion he baffled students by writing $f + a = o$ on the whiteboard and inviting students to give values to this odd little equation, and he asked them to think about it and give him an explanation by next time; at the end of the next lesson, he quickly lost patience with students who had no idea what values to ascribe to the equation. His idea was that a society governed by *fear* (*f*) and the desire to *appease* (*a*) alien forces or alien values would inevitably end up *oppressing* (*o*) its own people or its own values. He then proceeded to extend the equation, so that $f + a = o = dc$, where *dc* was supposed to represent *decline of civilisation*. If these schoolboy antics were designed to foster an interest in history, they failed miserably, because his students were unable to apply them, and they were unable to apply them because their knowledge of history was woefully inadequate; moreover, since these little asides had nothing whatever to do with pure mathematics, students concluded that they were simply time-wasters. Markus, however, seemed to think that his equations had about them the certainty of $E = MCxMC$, which led him to talk of the *continuity* of historical development, which, he maintained, was similar to continuity in mathematics; an equation which is valid today will be valid tomorrow if the values assigned to its components remain constant; *ceteris paribus*, what holds today will hold tomorrow. He quoted Frank, who in turn had quoted Percy: *Yesterday, the day before yesterday, and all our yesterdays, are one – and today is tomorrow's yesterday.* This aggravated matters, for it seemed to make as much sense to his students as an attempt to square the circle. Markus's asides were therefore considered not only irrelevant, but eccentrically so; eccentric or not, the whole experience was at least *unsettling*; the word had been used by the student himself when explaining matters to Rashid; when Rashid later approached Simon, he had only pretended to search for the right word, for he knew it well enough already, so well that he had rehearsed it and the word had been waiting, like a bloodhound on heat, to be released at precisely the right moment.

No doubt Percy would have been most impressed by the choice of the word 'unsettling'. He would have astutely remarked that it was a neutral word, in the sense that that it implied nothing at all about rightness or wrongness, logicality or illogicality, rationality or irrationality. The word connoted something psychological as distinct from logical, in that what unsettles may be either real or unreal, right or wrong – judgement about truth and falsity is, as it were, suspended. The word, one might say, stopped short of any kind of *debate*, and was therefore delightfully appropriate.

For debate implies doubt, doubt as to whether the subject of the debate was right or wrong, true or false; and doubt would imply a degree of reluctance to judge one way or the other until the matter is thoroughly investigated. It would also imply a maturity of mind, an openness of mind, a desire not to draw false conclusions; it would imply a considerable degree of intellectual integrity, which would, in turn, suggest probity, uprightness, honesty, a desire to set things straight, a desire to be right, to be truthful, to hide nothing. Intellectual integrity and moral integrity would blend together like the ingredients of a prize dinner for two in a five-star restaurant.

In short, free debate would imply everything that did not obtain in the circumstances in which people found themselves, in a society where fear ruled, in a society in which ISI governed people's lives. Percy had once read a line in a philosophy book written by Ludwig Wittgenstein, a man who had, he felt sure, something very important to say but was difficult to understand, *'The truth cannot come out when something else which charms one bars the way'*. Yes, that was the one line that he annotated in the margin, the one line he felt he could relate to. Many things may bar the way – fear, certainly, could do it. And the word 'unsettling' suggested fear – fear in the forced absence of debate; fear which, indeed, *necessitated* the forced absence of debate.

It followed, therefore, that whether Markus might be right or wrong, whether what he said to students was true or false, unreasonable or unreasonable, valid or invalid, was quite beside the point, simply because the integrity which doubt demands was quite absent. All that was required was to show that what he said was *unsettling*. And if it was *unsettling*, it followed, by a perversion, or rather *absence*, of logic, that it was also *wrong*.

*　*

While Rashid was intimidating Simon, Markus was reading a letter from Frank, who had promised to keep in touch. It read:

Dear Markus,

    I hope you have well and truly settled in to your new job by now. You must be in your element doing what you like best.

I must say, I miss our walks together – though, I'm ashamed to admit it, I didn't fully appreciate them at the time. Now I'm practically confined to my flat and manage to get around it with the help of my Zimmer – not exactly Formula One, I must say – but I just have to accept it. Well, growing old isn't easy, and accepting it gracefully, I find, is harder still. I spend a lot of time listening to music and looking out of the window. I used to enjoy watching the birds through my binoculars, but my eyesight isn't what it used to be, and the binoculars are heavy to hold up, so it's more a case of the birds watching me! I suppose I could get a pair with a tripod, but I can't be bothered. I used to enjoy watching television, but I'm finding it harder to focus – anyway, there's nothing stimulating to watch these days – just mediocrity and propaganda, as Percy would say (you remember I told you all about my old pal Percy?). It's amazing how things have changed. I'm reading again a book about a chap, a writer, by the name of Dennis Potter, and you can take it and read it yourself when you visit me – which I hope you will be able to do during one of your breaks. Anyway, Potter used to write amazing things, dramas, for television, really wonderful things, because he thought that television was the best way to reach people and to tackle themes that really matter. He thought you should 'fight and kick and bite' to get your material on television – oh, and that's the name of the book, by the way – it's a biography, and the author, W. Stephen Gilbert, says that Potter 'fiercely opposed the censorship of views and the repression of freedom of debate'. Oh, my! So different now, isn't it? All that's in the past, and I wouldn't know what to call it now. If Potter tried any of that stuff now, I suppose he'd be spending most of his time in a Rehabilitation Centre, or something much worse.

Seditious, they'd call it and they'd drag in that ISI business to stop him – assuming he'd ever get started at all. But maybe it's something more of us should do in life while we still can, television or no television – I mean, we should do much more fighting and kicking and biting, don't you think? Yes, I'm sure you agree.

I'm sorry if I'm rambling on. It's taken me all day to write this, my eyes being what they are, and I know I tend to go on a bit. Talking about writing, are you still writing in that notebook of yours? I hope so. It helps, I'm sure. You just need to be careful, that's all.

Just one last thing. I don't remember ever telling anyone else this, but I'd like to tell you about the time my father was on his deathbed. We were standing at his bedside – my mother, my sister and me – and he took and kissed our hands in turn, and then he said, 'Look after one another'. Now why did he say that? Well, you're the one with the brains – you can work it out. Anyway, you look after yourself, too.

I think I've tired myself out. Time to stop. Time for bed – again!

Yours ever,

Frank

P.S. I'm looking forward to seeing you again – hopefully with a nice girl in tow as well. Any chance of that yet?

Yes, Markus agreed, the letter was rather rambling, but, then, remarkably well put together for a man of his age. It was something to think about – the way that some people grew very old, still sharp in mind but weak in body, like Frank, while for others it went the other way, and Markus wondered whether it was really better to be weak all round, in mind as well as body. Frank was in a complaining mood – but his complaints were not at all ill-judged; perhaps ignorance was bliss and senility a saving grace, for then he would know nothing to complain about. What Markus did not know was that writing this kind of letter showed another kind of change – a change in Frank himself, from the quiet, unassuming individual he had been most of his life, almost obsessed with security and safety, to the more forceful, open and courageous author of an epistle that time alone had allowed him to write. Was it better to live like an animal grazing in a field, without the means to question the surroundings? Did happiness consist in ignorance? Or should we say, with John Stuart Mill, that it is better to be a Socrates dissatisfied than a pig satisfied? Markus decided that old Frank was, without equivocation, no pig. The letter proved it, which is why Markus read and re-read it many times in the days that followed, thinking even that it might be framed and stuck up on the wall, or that it should, in micro form, be inscribed on the foreheads of every student and, for that matter, every teacher, in that institution – that institution which had the temerity, and, above all, the ignorance, to call itself an institution of learning.

Markus's first thought was to seek out the book about Potter in the university library; his second thought, which was in fact quite correct, was that such a book as this about such a man as that would prove to be permanently unavailable. Censorship had become a flexible, not to say rubbery, tool, for it worked backwards as well as forwards, and work had long been underway to cleanse all libraries of unsettling material. Frank's copy was years old, and where he had picked it up he would not have been able to say. Maybe it had been one of Percy's castoffs, or one of the many books he had lent out and never got back. True, it was still possible to follow courses with the title Media Studies, in which the role of television and similar media were discussed, but 'discussions' consisted very largely of pale descriptions of the blandly obvious, and were anything but penetrating; innovations inside the media were frowned upon unless they aided and abetted social cohesion at any cost, and the cost was dreadfully high. Potter's first introduction to television had impressed him enormously; what had struck him most was the sheer *power* of this medium; he saw television as a liberating opportunity, something which might free people from what he considered the tyrannies of class, status and gutter-press ignorance; his was an optimism which he expressed in the phrase 'switch on, tune in and *grow*'. He had not of course been wrong about the power of television; but the corollary needed to be added to the equation, that it was a power that might be used for good or ill or nothing at all. Right now, the only growth it allowed was downward and backward on the sacrificial altar of social cohesion, giving as much irritation to integrity as an in-growing toenail gives to its wincing possessor. The media had long ago lost their heroes and, with them, all unsettling ideas.

16
SIP: Standard Interrogation Procedure

'You understand that we are required, by law, to follow up any complaints made that may affect you directly or indirectly? Oh, please sit down.'

Markus sat down on the plain, hard wooden chair that had been placed at the table, on the opposite side of which sat the customary committee of three, consisting of two stony-faced gentlemen in their late fifties, one apparently Asian, the other apparently as English as shepherd's pie, and a rather attractive, bespectacled black woman in her mid- to late forties. The shepherd's pie in the centre had spoken.

'Yes? You understand that?' and Markus nodded in the affirmative.

'What's the charge?'

'The charge?' the shepherd's pie momentarily discarded his stony face and, with a slight giggle, looked quickly at his companions on either side.

'Accusation, then.' Markus seemed to be playing with them – not that it was noticed.

'Well, hardly that, either,' the shepherd's pie went on, resuming his stony face. 'It's not our business to make charges or accusations. Our brief, as members of the Supervisory and Advisory Committee, is simply to, er, well look into, shall we say, any, well, for want of a better word, *abnormality* that may have arisen in the course of your working here for us.'

Markus felt a fleeting twitch of irritation, as he had always done so, at the suggestion that he was working for anyone other than the students under his immediate tutelage. He was not working for the university, not even for himself, and he was most certainly not working for SAC. He wanted to tell them that, to set things straight. But there was no time, not even time enough to formulate his objection, let alone articulate it.

'Yes, and it has been brought to our attention that many, *some*, of your remarks to your students are let us say, app... apposite.' The pie stumbled over the word, suggesting perhaps that his sentences had been rehearsed and that he was still uncertain of his script.

'Really? I am not aware of it.'

'You teach mathematics, pure mathematics, Dr Shelby?'

'Of course.'

'And yet, we have been told, by your own students no less, that you seem to be as much concerned about history as you are, or should be, about the subject you have been engaged to teach.' The pie smiled broadly, again with quick glances to left and right. 'Hopefully, Dr Shelby, you are not beginning to confuse the two!' The pie giggled, again glancing left and right.

'Not at all.'

'Good. So you are saying that these, er, complaints are unfounded – or at least wildly exaggerated.'

'Not exactly.'

'Not exactly?'

'I am engaged to teach mathematics, as you rightly say. This I do. But I want my students to think, to think for themselves. In my experience, and I include myself in this, people who have a flair for mathematics are not generally equally capable of taking a wider look round, especially in the country as it is today. I want them to take a wider look round – to be aware of what is happening around them, and to question what is happening. I thought that a few meaningful little games might do the trick – expressing some ideas in mathematical form might get them wondering, get them thinking, get them asking questions, so that they stop taking everything for granted, and ...'

'You said "the country as it is today". What do you mean exactly?' The apparently Asian gentleman had been taking notes and had heard nothing apart from this phrase. The question was Markus's cue. If it was bait, Markus took it – hook, line and sinker.

'All countries at all times have things wrong with them – but what is happening in this country now is particularly worrying – restrictions on free speech under the pretext of something called "political correctness" – even free thinking is something people are afraid to undertake, let alone teach. In fact, they have probably forgotten what free thinking means! Appeasement is taking the place of such liberties, the toleration of alien values, the adoption of ways of living, of mindsets that are alien to—'

'But you, Dr Shelby, are very free to express your opinions – as you are doing right now – and you're making the most of it, I'd say,' snapped the attractive black lady, who seemed now suddenly less attractive. Beauty, perhaps, is sometimes so fragile that it disappears when it has found a voice.

'That's because you have brought me here and want, I thought, to hear me out, but we have a wider responsibility—'

'Sometimes, Dr Shelby, we all need to make compromises. Be *reasonable*. Society is very different now from what it used to be, and we must all adjust to changing times. Yes, yes, it stands to reason.' The pie spoke, nodding slowly in time with the generally perceived wisdom of his own utterance.

'Well, there is all the difference in the world between reasonable compromise and stark appeasement at any cost, just as there is between the undisputed and the indisputable. I mean, just because something is unquestioned, it doesn't follow that it's unquestionable. So-called religious people don't question of the existence of their God, much to our cost – but that doesn't mean that the existence of their God is unquestionable, and the rest of us should do a lot more, yes a great deal more, to question it.'

'I hope you're not preaching religious intoleration, Dr Shelby,' said the apparently Asian gentleman, 'because if you are, it will not do – no, it will never do!'

'That was just an example. Do you know, a book called *The Vindication of the Rights of Woman* was published in 1792, yes, in the eighteenth century, and written by a woman. It was possible to talk of vindication then – but now it's fast becoming a crime to suggest equality between men and women! And as for homophobia – that's on the increase! And anti-Semitism, too! Oh, yes, all these things appear like monsters out of the deep as soon as we take a wider look around. Our society is going backwards at a rate of knots and—'

'Thank you, Dr Shelby! Thank you for that most edifying speech. However, we are not here either to give or to listen to speeches, edifying or not. Now, you understand that this committee is charged with the responsibility of reporting its findings to the Review Panel, and you will be hearing from them shortly, I have no doubt. In the meantime, may I very strongly suggest that you teach your students to think about mathematics, and mathematics *only*. Please ask yourself how your students can possibly be expected to make progress in such a difficult subject if their minds are distracted by matters that are utterly irrelevant to their course of study. Just ask yourself that!'

'I would like—'

'Ah, no, Dr Shelby. We have finished here. Please wait in the anteroom.'

Markus got up and left the room, feeling every bit like a recalcitrant student who has just been given a final warning – a warning given by people who knew nothing at all about mathematics and who were, quite clearly, blind to any suggestion that academic compartmentalism was a thing of the past, if it had ever existed at all except in the minds of its proponents, deaf to any recommendation that it should be relegated to the nursery of human development. His immediate feeling was that he had been a bad boy, but he quickly managed to shake the feeling off. And once he had shaken it off, he felt resentful to those who had made him feel that way in the first place. Resentment was mixed with shame; he was ashamed of himself for having embarrassed himself by opening up to people who were not, and could never possibly be, on the same wavelength as he; he had demeaned himself by offering an explanation for what was, or what ought to be, very obvious and without question commendable. Where was his pride? Better by far if he had donned a mantle of silence, like Christ before Pilate, and simply allowed the committee to condemn itself. But if he had been treated in the way that a schoolboy might be treated by bad teachers, and made to feel inadequate because his confidence had been undermined, he resolved to react not simply by playing the bad boy, but by becoming even worse – in fact, by becoming as bad as it was possible to be. Unfortunately, his resolution suffered from the further reflection that his own students had reported him. He was doubly in despair: he had tried to speak at length to a committee which was determined not to hear him, and all because he had wasted his time in the attempt to get his own students to think for themselves. He was also mortally offended, deeply insulted by the injunction that he should be *reasonable*; because reason was precisely his business, his domain; it was what mathematics and the critical appraisal of human development was all about; if there was any connection between history and mathematics, reason was the link; it was what thinking was all about, the drawing of conclusions, the making of comparisons, the perception of similarities and dissimilarities; it was what separated human beings from the beasts of the wilderness, human from animal and all things inanimate. He felt closer than ever to John the Baptist, a voice in a wilderness. He was abandoned; he had expected little or nothing from SAC; but he was apparently abandoned by his students, and, as for his fellow academics, he was determined not to hold his breath.

Such were his reflections in the anteroom. He was kept waiting there for more than an hour – ample time for second and third helpings of such thoughts.

Little did he know that he would not be given a final warning. Worse than that, his contract would be terminated with almost immediate effect. And even that was not to be the end of the matter. Once big balls of lead are set in motion, who can tell where they will land?

* *

Big balls of lead are one thing; historical development is quite another. Even so, if experimental conditions have been neatly tailored, the course taken by balls of lead may be predicted with some degree of certainty. And Percy and Markus would presumably have argued that, once the parameters are set and the variables are agreed, the course of historical events was as predictable as clockwork and could hold no surprises for the initiated.

While Markus was in the unenviable process of demeaning himself before Pilate, an agent of SAC had let himself into his rooms in the hope, if not the expectation, of finding incriminating evidence of recalcitrant and seditious activity or material. And since Markus's invitation to appear before the illustrious committee had come out of the blue, he had had no time to consider the possibility that his privacy might be intruded upon, and even less time to consider the possible ramifications of such an intrusion. His notebook with the blue cover and the letter from Frank were in full sight on his desk and were eventually found; their placement was so obvious and guileless that they were not discovered at first, and not before his bed had been turned over and put back again, and the cushions on his armchairs and the books in his bookcase had all been displaced.

Which would explain why, directly after his appearance before SAC, he was asked to wait in an anteroom, ensuring that there was sufficient time for the agent to do his work and return. They then sifted through the evidence, which had been hurriedly placed on their desk in a large brown paper envelope, and quickly assessed how damning it was. And just how damning they considered it to be was demonstrated by their immediate recommendation, by telephone, to the Review Panel that his contract with the university should be terminated.

'Oh, do sit down Dr Shelby.' Markus had been ushered before the committee again, and the words emanated from the pie. 'Oh, yes, you recognise it, do you? You look rather shocked. I suppose we should apologise for having had to intrude on your privacy. But, as you will of course appreciate, it is very much our business to delve into other people's affairs – all in the best interests of the university, of the students – er, not to say of society at large. No! We'd like to hold on to that – for the time being.' Markus had made to take his notebook, recognising at the same time the letter from Frank.

'I must say, it all makes for quite dismal reading, and I – we – can see more clearly why your students find things unsettling – most unsettling. Yes, it suggests to us that you are – let us say – a round peg in a square hole, Dr Shelby. Not quite at home here. No, not at all. In view of this we have unanimously decided to advise the Review Panel accordingly. They will of course make their own decision, but it is only fair to tell you now that the prospects of your continuing in this establishment are rather grim.'

Markus was silent, not so much because he was given a second chance to play Jesus hauled before Pilate and was determined to go through with it, but simply because he was stunned. Stunned into inactivity like a rabbit in the headlights of an oncoming vehicle. In terms of his own belief, thanks to Percy, of the inevitable, quasi-mathematical, certainty of the continuity of historical events, one might even say that he was shocked by the validity of his own theory. The theory of continuity worked only too well, it seemed. For here was Socrates again, condemned whatever he said – as good, in fact, as condemned *in absentia*. Here was Thomas More, condemned by his own words of innocence, naively believing that where there is no malice there can be no crime, and demonstrating what he might have said – that the aristocracy of England would snooze through the Sermon on the Mount; here was George Fox, judged guilty before he opened his mouth, and whose brilliant words of justification turned out to be no more and no better than going through the motions; here was Enoch Powell, who had learned the hard lesson that it will not do to give people the truth on a plate, for they will find it indigestible and spit it back in your face. It was as though Markus had made himself a guinea pig in an experiment of his own making and was astonished by the outcome; but whether he should be elated by having established the validity of his own theory was not a question he was capable of entertaining. However his silence is to be explained, silent he was, and silent he remained.

He was told that the committee had now completed their inquiries and that he was free to go. Which was not altogether true. He was also told that his effects, that is, notebook and letter, would be returned. That was not altogether true, either. What had already returned, however, was the feeling that he had been caught with his hand in the jam jar, as if he should exclaim 'It's a fair cop 'guv!', the feeling that he had been a bad boy and had been caught red-handed, as if to invalidate, or at least counteract, the resolution he had made during his long wait in the anteroom. Had he begun to doubt the validity of his own resolution? Had he begun to doubt his own sanity? Could one be shocked into insanity? One could, it seemed, be shocked into doubting the sanity of everyone else – making it hard to hold on to one's own.

The wind blew rough that night, blowing the loose tops off refuse bins and causing dry leaves to rattle like rattlers on pavements and down country lanes; not a night for dreamless sleep; even the innocent failed to rest easy; and for those who were found guilty of innocence it was a night deserving a place in some fantastical horror story, too shocking for the young and too disturbing for the old. And for those who hovered on the border of sanity and insanity, the wind echoed their unrest and made it uncertain which side of the dark ravine they would find themselves in the morning light. Markus lay listening to the relentless howling of the wind, and thinking of the Hand of Fate: a man has plans, a path ahead of him, everything in a straight line; and then, out of nowhere, he meets someone, or something happens, and everything he had in mind is turned inside-out, and the path he had thought straight develops twists and turns, and perhaps bends back on itself, and all is suddenly alien, all plans flattened, and even the drawing-board on which those plans were written is irretrievably lost. And then one feels compelled to ask, 'Why?' Suppose he had not met Frank, and Frank had not told him about Percy … what then? And then, on the other hand, did such questions really matter?

* *

While Markus was tossing and turning in obedience to the dictates of the wind, Frank lay in bed listening to the silence that reigned in his neck of the woods; no winds blew there that night; on the contrary, the night was still as a corpse, so still that Frank was himself restless on account of it. He thought of the cruel stillness that accompanies the dead when their voices can no longer be heard and of the loneliness that this silence engenders in those that loved them and live on. It was on such a night that Frank's father passed to the other side; an unnatural silence had enveloped the event, a booming silence, such a silence that seemed to fill the air with its presence, causing those who grieved to tremble and mourn. His thoughts were in a state of flux, as they moved from his father to his grandmother, whom he felt he had neglected as a young man, for in youth people think far less of the old and the past than they do of the young and what is to come. He remembered how, so many years later when he himself was old, he had made a ridiculous attempt to make up for that neglect by making the journey to his grandmother's grave, while his legs could still bear his weight. He had stood at the graveside and apologised to his grandmother for not having visited her more often all those years ago, as though she could hear him and would perhaps forgive him; for if she heard him, she would most certainly forgive him; but did she hear him? As he stood at her graveside, he imagined her round and kindly face smiling up at him from deep down, and he felt his tears struggling to free themselves, and, because he felt the struggle, the tears multiplied and ran in mini-rivulets. People who mean so much must be kept close, for they cannot be replaced, and neglect can never be made good. All were gone now. Yes, all gone – even Henry, and Percy – and his beloved Sal! Oh, Lord, the weight of memory! And then … Markus came to mind. Markus must have received the letter. Frank hoped that he had received it safely. Hopefully he would reply – when, of course, he had the time; Markus was busy making a life of his own, but doubtless, well, again, hopefully, he would keep in touch.

Markus would, of course, need to watch his step and keep in line, for life now was fully of snares; on the other hand, Frank's feelings had become ambivalent on this question of personal security; for he was glad he'd told Markus about Percy and that Markus seemed to be of a similar questioning, delving and critical disposition. What was it Percy had said? Yes, that's it: children should dream their dreams, though vague and half-baked; the young should be allowed to hope; old men should warn; and everyone should proceed with at least a modicum of caution. Percy spoke about the young faces in the classroom; faces unlined, and heads full of bubbles which would burst soon enough – it was criminal to disabuse them of their fairy stories; but for men there was no excuse. Frank thought of Potter again, and the phrase 'fight and kick and bite' seemed to suggest what good men should do when faced with the injustices and follies that seemed to dog, if not dominate, man's plodding existence here on earth. He now remembered that it was indeed Percy who had lent him that book about Potter. Poor Percy.

17
The New Archipelago

Things had moved on apace since Percy's demise, and all in the name of simplification and facilitation; these two principles had been twinned together and had formed a slippery slope towards an inevitable dehumanisation of social institutions. SAC, for example, although initially given the limited remit of having to advise university Review Panels, could now refer difficult cases directly to a local Office of Correction, and, in turn, OCs were empowered to refer such cases to Rehabilitation Centres. For SAC to make its referrals, all that was necessary was the unanimous agreement of the three members of the committee in question; similarly, the unanimous agreement of the three magistrates of the Office of Correction was sufficient to incarcerate the hapless subject in a Rehabilitation Centre. Indeed, even for serious criminal cases outside the scope of ISI, cases deemed to be outside the gambit of sedition and social incohesion, such as murder and burglary and robbery, unanimity amongst a small committee or panel of appointees had taken the place of the jury system of old. The jury system had long ago been abandoned for being awkward, cumbersome, long-winded and unreliable; first it was decided that the jury system could no longer be considered fit for purpose in view of the increasing complexity of cases, in particular cases concerning computer fraud and computer hacking; small select committees replaced juries; but this proved to be the thin end of the wedge, and the principles of simplification and facilitation were applied across the board.

Given the ever-widening scope of ISI, SACs and OCs came to play an increasingly important role in the archipelago of the judicial system. *Political correctness* had itself started out as little more than an irritating socio-political affliction, but the idea had spawned the development of *political correction,* a much more forthright and sinister development which carried life-changing, if not life-ending, consequences for those who infringed the rules of political correctness; for those who infringed them were subject to ISI.

The webs we make, or those that are made for us, on our behalf and even for own perceived welfare, are therefore capable of extension and of ensnaring the very people they are intended to protect. In this vast web-like archipelago, it was perfectly possible for an individual subject to its rigours to effectively 'disappear', thus obviating the need to restore capital punishment. Either the subject reformed to the satisfaction of his judicial benefactors, or he was passed to a Rehabilitation Centre in which he could, at least in theory, be rehabilitated and freed, or else he could be detained indefinitely and thus 'disappear' and become no longer a threat either to himself or to the rest of humanity, and in this way, his disappearance might be said to secure social cohesion. For those inside the archipelago of the penal system, fixed-term sentences were a thing of the past.

It might be thought that such an efficient system of netting and incarceration would bring to bear impossible demands in terms of numbers, so that Rehabilitation Centres would need to be increased *ad infinitum,* and that since no increase can proceed to infinity, the system must inevitably collapse. Not so, however. For the system engendered such a degree of fear and foreboding, fear of disappearing and never again emerging to the light of day, that numbers remained, though very high, at least manageable. The system was retainable provided fear could be relied upon; therefore, the propagation of fear and foreboding was a principle that went hand in hand with the twin principles of simplification and facilitation – as a house of cards depends for its longevity on the counter-forces at work amongst the cards themselves; a house of cards might collapse from a shock external to it. That shock had not come, had not *yet* come, and was not expected to come, to the archipelago. Altogether, the system was extremely effective, kept in place by fear and dread of the Rehabilitation Centres, which, it was known, or if not known then certainly *surmised*, had as little to do with rehabilitation as The Flat Earth Society had to do with astrological veracity.

* *

Frank lay awake in the stillness of that night, shifting this way and that, like a man in the discomfort of pain believing, of course wrongly, that if only he could move onto the other side everything would be alright. Needless to say, he did not feel his best first thing in the morning, which explains his unusual irritation when someone had the temerity to knock on his door. Frank shuffled towards the door with his Zimmer; clearly not fast enough to prevent a second bout of knocking, appreciably louder than the first – which did not tend to improve Frank's humour.

'Mr Russell? Frank Russell?' The voice belonged to a portly gentleman, moustached and bespectacled, who held a clipboard close to his chest as though it were additional protection against the cutting chills of early morning. 'Masters. Adrian Masters – the LHA? Just a check-up. See if you're alright. Just routine.' Masters wore a blue lanyard round his neck with his name card attached; he held the card up to Frank's face – pointlessly, for Frank had not the time to try to make it out.

It needs to be explained that the penal system was not the only archipelago then extant whose complexity defied simple description, despite the fact that all archipelagos were devised to serve the interests of the twin principles of simplification and facilitation. The National

Health Service, as Frank had known it as a small boy, had long ago died the death of a thousand cuts, and the health of the nation was now devolved on Local Health Authorities (LHAs). Tragically, but in keeping with the ethos of the times, the LHAs were more concerned with keeping sickness and destitution off the streets and under the carpet than it was with curative medicine; preventative medicine had been long ago relegated to the nursery of dreams and belonged to a distant and far more illuminated past.

It was highly improbable, but not altogether implausible, that Frank should receive a visit from the LHA. But this early in the morning? Frank was faced with a stark and immediate choice: either to close the door on the poor fellow, who stood there shivering in his boots, or to let him in; so it was with a grunt and a nod that he shuffled aside to let the man inside, out of the biting cold. Masters walked ahead into the living room with a sprightly step, as though he felt quite at home, and stood in the middle of the room, his eyes darting here and there as though he were about to take an inventory.

'Tea?'

'No – well, yes, yes, if that's alright.' Masters laid his clipboard on the table and his gloves on the sideboard behind him, and then he made a beeline for Frank's bookcase while Frank was busy making a pot of tea in the adjoining kitchen. 'A lot of books, Mr Russell,' he said – but Frank didn't hear.

'You've quite a few books, Mr Russell,' he said, as Frank slowly negotiated his way to the table, without the aid of his Zimmer.

'Here, let me help with that!' Masters took the tea tray from Frank and placed it on the table. 'Shall we sit here? Do you read a lot, then?'

'Not so much these days – my eyes won't let me.'

'Yes, well, as I said, this is just a routine visit – to find out, basically, if you have any special needs. Do you?'

'Special needs – well, no, really.' Frank smiled inwardly. Everyone has special needs, and Frank had his, but he'd be damned if he would say what they were.

'You're comfortable using your Zimmer frame, then?'

'Well, it's not much use if you want to carry something … I don't always use it. Helps to take the strain off my back and legs.'

'You mentioned your eyes.'

'Yes, not very good.'

'So, how do you spend your day – I mean, a typical day? Oh, I see you've a pair of binoculars!'

'Oh, not any more. I used to watch the birds from the window.'

'That window?' said Masters, pointing.

'You can see a huge variety of birds from there – and in the distance, on the tall trees across the fields, you can see crows and …' Frank stopped short, thinking of the debate he had had with Percy and Henry about what kind of binoculars he should buy, and Henry's joke that Frank didn't have to spend much on travel, because all the travelling he wanted to do was right under his own nose.

'Why?' asked Masters.

'Why?'

'Yes, why did you watch the birds?' The question seemed ridiculous.

'Birds are fascinating creatures – the forms they take, the colours, their habits, their modes of flight. Haven't you seen them fly? And when they fly in flocks? All in the same direction, all at the same time, and all without getting in each other's way – they're free, and the freedom of one doesn't hurt the freedom of others … But you must know all this – haven't you ever watched them?'

'Well, I don't make a habit of it. Anyway, how do you spend your day now? You don't watch the birds because your eyesight isn't so good, yes?'

'Yes, I told you. And the binoculars are too heavy.'

'So how do you spend your day now? I don't suppose you write anything – I mean if your eyes ...'

'Write? God, no! Well, only short notes – and then with difficulty. It's not just my eyes – my hands can't hold a pen, not for long, and I've never been good at keyboards – no, writing's not for me.'

'So ...'

'Oh, for goodness sake – I just potter about, sit near the window, listen to music, think about the past ...' Frank was ruffled.

'About the past?'

'Of course – doesn't everyone?' There was no response from Masters, who seemed to be placing ticks in boxes on the paper stuck to his clipboard.

'One last question, Mr Russell: do you live alone?'

'Utterly. Oh, I have some help with the housework – that's all.'

'You have some friends, of course.'

'*Had*, yes. All gone now. I'll be joining them soon enough.'

'Oh, no, Mr Russell, I'm sure you've still got lots to look forward to – a lot of years in you yet' – at which Frank smiled feebly. Such lies people told – and not always to genuinely comfort and console, for they talked by rote, like a machine activated by a button.

'Right!' said Masters, ostensibly aiming another tick at a presumably appropriate box, and adding, *'No special needs.'* 'Well, I think that's all, Mr Russell – I'm sorry to have troubled you, especially this early in the morning. But we're very busy, you know, in our department – lots of calls to make – must make a start somewhere. No, no, I can see myself out – oh, and thanks for the tea!'

Masters left as quickly as he had entered. Perhaps it was true that he had a lot to do that day and had to make an early start. Frank had not got up but remained sitting at the table, his empty cup held in both hands, as if savouring the warmth of the cup while it still lasted. He was thinking of Henry and Percy, and then, and above all, Sal. Memories had been triggered, damn it.

It was not until midday that Frank noticed a pair of gloves on the sideboard, left in his haste by – now what was his name?

Frank looked up the appropriate departmental number in his telephone book. 'Yes, that's right. Master, no Masters – a Mr Adrian Masters, I believe it was. He's from your department. Came this morning and left his gloves here. Could you please—' Frank was asked to hold the line. And, a few moments later, received the extraordinary response: 'You must be mistaken – there is no one of that name in this department.' Frank wanted to insist … but the line went dead.

Frank put the gloves in a drawer and their mysterious owner at the back of his mind. The gloves would remain deep in the drawer, out of sight, but not out of mind, for their owner, though never seen again, would continue to haunt Frank's waking hours.

*　*

The file on Frank Russell in the regional Office of Correction was extremely thin. Stamped on the front of it were the words '*No Further Action Required. RS only.*' Given his age and circumstances, he was very fortunate to be the subject of no more than 'Routine Surveillance' – which would be conducted with the utmost discretion and at a decent distance.

18
The Invisibles

Who Adrian Masters was, or really was, and whether in fact his name was Adrian Masters, were the thoughts which puzzled Frank in the days and months ahead. He wanted to tell Markus all about it, but he had already written one letter, and it was physically painful to write another; and even if he did tell him all about it, it might get him into trouble. No, it would be far better to wait until Markus had an opportunity to visit him and then, no doubt, they could while away many an hour theorising this way and that. He would show Markus the gloves, for they were incontrovertible evidence that Frank had not imagined it all, for it would not be the first time that old men in their dotage had fantasised about things. And so the days passed, one after another, and still no word from Markus – not even a quick telephone call – although, truth to tell, telephone calls were as painful, if not more so, than writing, for Frank's hearing was none too good, either; he avoided making telephone calls and dreaded receiving them. No, a letter, even very short, would be best. But still no word. Still no word.

Days became weeks, and weeks were in danger of transmuting into months, until, at last, Frank could bear it no longer. He was finally moved to telephone the university switchboard, ask for the relevant faculty and politely request to be put through to Dr Markus Shelby who, he surmised, must have an office of his own. Markus had never given him his number, and Frank had never asked for it; but then, he had never thought he would have such urgent need of it; no matter, hassle or no hassle, he determined to do the deed.

He found no difficulty reaching the switchboard; it took a little longer to get through to the faculty – and Frank came to wish that he had never got through to the faculty at all, indeed that he had never bothered to telephone at all. After being kept waiting for what seemed an unbearable age, he was told that he could not be put through to Dr Shelby, simply because Dr Shelby had 'moved on' and no longer taught there; moreover, and astonishingly, the faculty could give him no forwarding address or number. It was as though Markus had ceased to exist. It was no use trying to get sense from the other end; it was hard enough to hear clearly what was being said. Frank put down the handset with an unpalatable mixture of physical relief and emotional anguish. The whole thing was so unexpected and so ridiculous – could it possibly be that he had imagined everything? Had Markus existed at all? Was he a figment of Frank's warped and demented imagination? Markus … Adrian Masters … Perhaps it was all … Frank shook his head vigorously, as if to bring himself back to his senses. 'Well, Frank, you may be much less than the man you were … You may be at the end of your time here … But it can't be that bad. No, it just can't be.'

Eventually, such feelings of self-doubt wore off, like demons put to flight, allowing reason to return, or as much reason as Frank was able to muster. No, the more rational explanation was that Markus had indeed moved on, and a girl might have been at the bottom of it – who knows? Or perhaps he hadn't got on well with some of his colleagues; or perhaps he had simply been offered a better position – rather soon, but such things do happen. With such thoughts Frank sought to console himself and bring his ship back on course. And the thing to do now was to wait – Markus would one day reveal all, all in his own good time, yes, all in his own good time. In any case, one had to wish the best for him. After all, it wasn't as if he and Markus were related in any way at all; and then there was the age gap to consider – why on earth should Frank, really a stranger, expect a young man like Markus, with the whole world in front of him, to keep regularly in touch or, for that matter, to keep in touch at all? No wonder that people like Adrian Masters spoke by rote – after all, people who don't know each other, who have no real stake in each other, tend to communicate in clichés – that's what they do – perfectly normal, and it was wrong to expect anything different. So Frank began to question his expectations. He was expecting far too much from Markus – even from the likes of Adrian Masters.

With such reflections, Frank managed to lull himself into a more settled, less questioning state of mind. And in the course of time, fact and fiction, reality and unreality seemed to edge closer together. The time indeed would come when, in Frank's poor head, Markus Shelby became Adrian Masters, and Adrian Masters became Percy, and Percy became Henry, and Frank? Well, a time when even Frank was no longer at all sure of himself, or indeed of anything else; Frank, like many others, would one day be assailed by one long, dreamlike, fuzzy mass of recollection merging together, invading the present and then retreating from it, and invading it again. Perhaps it was Nature's way of putting to rest puzzles which he would never be able to solve – until that day when Nature, hopefully in kindly mood, gently closes the door and shuts out every light – as it did while Frank was sitting in his armchair gazing out of the window, listening to Bach's *Chaconne in D minor*.

* *

It was not therefore given to Frank to know the fate of the Invisibles. Frank, like all men, became subject to an eternal silence not of his own making. Markus had, at length and after putting up the stoutest defence he could muster, decided that silence was just as effective. The very idea of defence had struck him as faintly ludicrous, because, for him, what he was asked to defend was an evident as $2+2=4$, and how does one defend that? How does one defend a proposition like this, one without which one can't even get started? But, he reflected, from time immemorial great things have been said which have fallen on deaf ears, and great things done which hardly get a mention. He had managed to get hold of a book on the political oratory of ancient Greece, and he remembered the very first lines of the *Panegyricus* of Isocrates, published in about 380 BC: *The institution of festivals which often include athletic competitions has often led me to feel surprise at the large rewards offered for mere physical successes, while the unselfish endeavour of men who have set their whole being to work for the benefit of others receives no recognition, though they merit the greater consideration.*

Markus also remembered something else. Isocrates was well aware that the point he was making was far from original and also aware of the danger of repeating to an audience things they had heard before. But the themes he was addressing were so important that the answer, he thought, was not to drop them altogether in search of new ones, but rather to tackle the same themes in a different way. Each person who had both the goodness and the talent to address such themes should try his hand at doing so. Originality lay in the approach to such themes, not in the themes themselves. It was a question of 'same horse, different rider', which was further proof of historical continuity – unsurprisingly, since human nature had changed little from the time of Isocrates to the day when Markus was absorbed into the labyrinth of the penal archipelago.

But Markus pursued a policy of silence, not because he had lost faith in the themes he wished to address, nor because he believed he lacked the talent to address them. If he had lost faith, he had lost it in the audience he was addressing; and once he admitted the possibility that the audience he was addressing was, despite their human physiognomy, substantially less than human, silence seemed to be the order of the day; he distinguished, as it were, between humanness and humanity and felt forced to concede the unwelcome, not to say tragic, and not to say dangerous, proposition that the former may be retained though the latter is lost. He concluded that human beings had themselves mutated, that they had become enveloped in a downward spiral from which there was no return – they had retained human form, but had become a mere empty shell of humanity. If true, there was little point addressing themes they could not comprehend, quite irrespective of how one tried to address them. Whether the silence he chose may be considered better or worse than the eternal silence which Frank had not chosen is perhaps an imponderable, but it has to be said that Markus had not surrendered his own humanity, and that he therefore suffered the loneliness that accompanies it in a world in which it has become unwelcome, a world which has become insane. But such thoughts are dangerous for he who thinks them. He was a stranger, if not to himself, then at least to all and sundry. This way, Lear had warned, madness lies, and at times Markus felt that the insanity might be his own, or that he was, by almost imperceptible degrees, imbibing the insanity of others. Like Frank, he was beginning to feel fact and fiction, reality and unreality merge. He fought against his own decline, even to the point of repeating his name over and over again, 'My name is Markus Shelby', 'My name is Markus Shelby'. Sleep, when it came, was his greatest ally. But there is only so much that sleep can do.

One can only imagine how distraught Frank would have been to know of Markus's fate. The sentiment of John Stuart Mill, 'It is better to be a Socrates dissatisfied than a pig satisfied', is rightly praised by the wise. But sometimes ignorance is bliss.

Sad to say, therefore, Markus was destined to become one of the Invisibles, amongst whose august assembly we might include the writers of articles and books which very few read and fewer still can read well; those who say such wise things and on such weighty matters that few have dreamed of or ever will – books and articles that find their weary way into dusty second-hand shops and are, at best, recycled into the trash of mediocrity. Perhaps the voices of the Invisibles can be heard only in the cold winds that blow across the hills in this green and pleasant land – green and pleasant still, despite the idiocies which are played out upon it. What mournful but irresistible sounds these voices make when they sing in chorus, blowing as they do through the uncomprehending grass, ruffling the wool on the backs of the sheep that graze there, and whistling through the leaves that rustle in orchestral unison. These voices may still be heard by those capable of hearing them, despite the clamour of mediocrity, despite a world in which honours fall from the air like confetti and are just as enduring as these little paper flakes of snow.

19

Mary Had a Little Lamb

Some years later, long after the demise of Frank Russell and when Dr Markus Shelby was no longer capable of asking who he was, DAS (Dissident Archives Section) was given the task by the regional Office of Correction of sorting dissident files. Those files stamped 'Do Not Destroy' had already been removed for more permanent and electronic safekeeping; it simply remained to sort the rest into piles, making sure that none were similarly marked and mistakenly overlooked. All files not bearing that stamp and older than five years were to be binned and then incinerated. It was simply a matter of continuing to ensure the simplification and facilitation of the filing system, of ensuring that material of insufficient importance was ditched, for it was time and energy consuming to transfer material from paper to electronic form. More cynically, of course, such 'cleansing' was also a step in the gradual process of allowing dissidents to fade from view – the process of gradual disappearance.

The job of carrying stuff in boxes to the binning area was given to a young man, a tall, thin, clean-shaven, red-haired college undergraduate who was killing time in the summer break. The day was like any other day in late July, rather hot and stuffy indoors, while outside it was cloudless and the occasional bird still sang. It was a day that would be remembered very clearly by the young man. Not that he would remember it as the day that the statue of Winston Churchill was pulled down in Parliament Square; feelings against Churchill had been running quite high; it was felt that by opposing Hitler's peace entreaties with Britain, Churchill had made war inevitable, and that his opposition to Hitler had given a fundamentally mistaken boost to Judaism; in addition, Churchill had said some pretty unwelcome things about Islam, calling it a creed rather than a religion, and a creed that posed a danger to civilisation. The anti-Churchill lobby had grown from a rivulet into a raging torrent. It became inevitable that his statue would be pulled down; and pulled down it was, to the accompaniment of a large, cheering crowd. The young man was not there to see it, and had he watched the news that evening, it would have seemed a quite unremarkable day, and the reference to the destruction and removal of Churchill's memorial statue was extremely matter-of-fact: *Today, in Parliament Square, the Statue of Winston Churchill was finally removed, drawing a large crowd of onlookers*. And that was that.

No, the young man remembered the day for quite a different, though some might say not entirely unconnected, reason. While carrying a box, full to the very brim, of documentation to be binned, some of the stuff on the top slipped off onto the highly polished floor of the corridor. The young man stopped, laid the box on the floor and began to gather the stuff that had fallen out. His eyes fell upon a notebook with a blue cover, which had slipped effortlessly out of *Dissident File No. MS 352086*. He quickly flicked through the book, and his attention was drawn to the last page, and to the last sentence on that page, and to the way in which the sentence was written:

*Mary had a little lamb – whose name was **Liberty! Of course! LIBERTY!***

The young man was intrigued. What could it possibly mean? Was it some kind of puzzle? Perhaps there were other things in the notebook that might explain it. The young man determined to take the book home, and quickly stuffed it under his shirt where it was held in place by the belt of his trousers, and there it remained all day. There were indeed many things in the notebook – things about people called Frank, and Percy, and Henry. And strange things about mathematics and equations and history, and the importance of words; yes, it would take time to read, and time to piece it all together, because it was not all nicely connected prose – and there were words like 'continuity' which needed some explanation, and there was something about fighting and kicking and biting – all very mysterious; mysterious, and deeply intriguing. The young man was determined to make sense of it, because he had never seen anything like it before. His university course was dry in comparison – everything about his course was simple and you just had to learn things by rote and spit them out again in examinations – there was no room for questions, no interesting questions, anyway. But the notebook with the blue cover was something else, something quite different, for it seemed to beg questions quite different from the straightforward, factual questions he was accustomed to being asked in examinations. It was a challenge and one that he looked forward to, a challenge he would address in his private hours – and, who knows? – he might also show it to some friends. But first, it was all his.

* *

I confess, it was a turning point in my life – finding the notebook with the blue cover – and by accident, too – well, if it really *was* an accident. It's enough to make one believe in such a thing as Fate. Or, should I say Destiny? I read it, insofar as it is possible to read such things, and I re-read it many times, and I still read it, over and over again. I have not yet found anyone to share it with – no one I can trust enough to call a friend, a *true* friend. Perhaps, one day …

20
The Christmas Room

That day never came. I am no longer that young man. Many years have passed. No, that day never came, not always because I trusted no one, for there were some that I did trust absolutely and entirely, but because I feared for the safety of those I loved. My wife and two boys, for example; of course I trusted them with all my heart, but I could do nothing that might compromise them. The notebook with the blue cover remained, and still remains, a secret; my wife has passed on, poor, poor dear, and my two boys are far away – and busy making lives of their own, as the saying goes. Now I live alone, and the secret lives with me, as it always has and always will.

But there is another secret, just as precious and just as dangerous. It is now a week before Christmas, or what people used to call by that name, and I am preparing the Christmas Room. It all started when I was a child living just with my mother, my father having died. My mother would say that we need to prepare the Christmas Room; the room was the smallest bedroom, at the rear of the house, well hidden from the road at the front, overlooking the garden where stood our solitary but beautiful copper beech tree, bereft in winter of its leaves but still grand and full of future promise; it stood proud and steadfast despite being solitary, alone and unsupported and buffeted by the winds and storms that Nature hurled its way – and yet grander for all that.

'It's time to get the Christmas Room ready,' my dear mother would say. 'But remember, Harry my dear, don't say a word to anyone! Promise?' 'Yes, mummy, I promise,' I would reply, uncomprehendingly. It was the same every year at this time, and after a few years I would ask her why it had to be a secret. She told me that many years ago this time would be celebrated by everyone but that little by little people stopped doing so, and that finally no one did; in fact, celebrating Christmas was at first frowned upon, and then, as if by magic, Christmas ceased to exist altogether, and then some law was passed to say that people caught celebrating Christmas would be punished. She said that it was connected with the idea that drinking alcohol was wicked, and some people started to say that Christianity was the wrong religion and should be suppressed completely. I must say, I failed to understand any of this very well. But apparently there was another religion which was regarded as superior in some way, and people followed that instead.

Explanations apart, as a child I relished helping my mother to prepare the small Christmas Room. She would make a little tree out of coloured paper; and the coloured paper left over, which I think she called 'trimmings', would hang here and there from the ceiling. It was such fun. Then she would sit me down and tell me about puddings, and strange things called 'crackers' which two people had to pull apart and which would go bang; she would tell me about Christmas trees much grander than our little paper tree, which had lights on them, lights which would come on and go off again, like twinkling stars; and she would tell me about special songs called 'carols', which she said she loved so much, and she would actually play some carols on an ancient cassette-recorder, though, of course, she would keep the volume very low, just in case someone somehow heard them and reported us – because then our wonderful secret would be out and we might be punished. And she would tell me about Christmas dinners, and party games, and laughter and smiles, and how, because they were happy, people would think more deeply about others who were not so fortunate as they; she tried to explain how Christmas was a bitter-sweet time, a time of sadness born out of happiness, but precious all the same, perhaps because of that, because it threw into relief the sufferings of others by heightening the awareness of those who cared. 'It's hard to find anyone who's happy, truly happy, now,' she would sigh. 'Happiness is not for our time, it seems.' I didn't understand this very well, either. But when she sighed, I sighed, too – at least, inwardly. She told me that long, long ago people would greet each other with 'Happy Christmas'; now, of course, it's 'Happy Holiday', or more often nothing at all. She would tell me, too, about Christmas cards, with painted scenes of snow and people singing carols under street lamps. She would talk about the times it would snow, and the sound the snow made underfoot, so that your steps were crunchy, and how you might go to bed with the grass green and wake in the morning to find a carpet of white snow, as if a wizard had waved his wand. But now it never snowed in winter, and I longed to see what it was like – to see a magic white carpet. Where had the magic gone? Oh, where? And would it ever come back?

She told me about holly; and about mistletoe, under sprigs of which people used to kiss – something unthinkable, indeed punishable, now. Kissing under mistletoe – was this magical, too? It sounded a little like a magical rite – if so, this was another piece of magic that had long been made to disappear.

But there was at least one piece of magic that my mother reserved for me alone. On what she called Christmas Morning, she would tell me to look under the little tree; and there would always be a small packet with my name on it and a present inside; she tried to convince me that it had been left there by someone called Father Christmas, who, she said, had put it there surreptitiously the night before. But even when very young, I challenged that assertion – after all, if such a person had really put it there, our little secret would be out, and I found that possibility frightfully unsettling. On this point, therefore, my mother had been hoist with her own petard.

And when the Christmas Room was ready, we would sit comfortably in that little room and listen to carols played softly, and sometimes we would hum along, or even sing the words – but never too loudly. After each session, my mother would wrap up the cassette carefully in a paper bag, as though it were made of the thinnest glass and might break under the slightest pressure, and when at last the Christmas Room was abandoned until the next Christmas, the tree and trimmings would be taken down and disposed of, so that no evidence of our little celebration remained, as though we had committed a capital crime and were busy destroying every vestige of the corpse, every shred of possibly incriminating evidence.

Time passed, and my poor mother passed with it, like a leaf swept away downriver. I had a family and a house of my own. But I said nothing about the Christmas Room. I dared not, for fear of compromising them. But now that I am alone, I shall prepare the smallest room at the rear of my own house and make it my Christmas Room, and I shall make my little tree, just as my mother did, and play her cassette of carols, which I too have been just as careful to keep safe. But will I be equally careful to keep the volume as low as possible? I don't know. I am tempted to play these carols as loudly as possible, come what may. But, as I say, I don't know. I would like to do it. I would like to do it very much. Very much indeed.

As for the demise of Christmas in this once green and pleasant land, the notebook with the blue cover has helped me to understand a little more than I did before. According to the notebook, people called Puritans abolished the celebration of Christmas in the seventeenth century, when the leader of the country was someone called Oliver Cromwell – which is strange, because the history books, or, rather, I should say, the one history book I managed at long last to find, tells us that this man relished his food and his drink and even his pipe; and his wife even wrote a little recipe book, so she and her husband no doubt delighted in the dishes she prepared. Perhaps he was beguiled in some way by forces that overwhelmed him – perhaps he was obliged to go with the flow. The notebook says that such things happen – that things, sometimes very bad things, begin in simple, even innocent, ways and end by bewitching us all. Is this what the notebook means by the 'continuity of history'? But the Puritans did not abolish Christmas, only the celebration of Christmas, because they believed that over-eating and over-drinking was not the way to celebrate the life and teachings of Jesus Christ. That I suppose is the essential difference between then and now. It seems that we might attribute the abolition of Christmas to the forces that we allow to overwhelm us. 'Christmas' is of course just a word, and they can erase the word; but can the meaning of the word be erased, too? But then, meanings can be forgotten, and when the meanings are good, forgetting them is bad, perhaps even tragic. And even if the word is retained, its meaning can still be forgotten, or it can come to mean something else, something better, or, more often something worse. Words and their meanings are all we have – that's what it says in the notebook with the blue cover. I can't quite understand it – but, yes, if words are all we have, we had better choose them carefully and be clear about what they mean, without at the same time defining them out of existence or making them subject to the death of a thousand cuts. I suppose it's also true that people have been either saved or condemned by words – by the words they use or those that are used by others. It's all very confusing, and I'm too old now to be confused by such things – or perhaps, not old enough! But these are just words, too.

* *

Well, I shall sit in my armchair in the Christmas Room and listen to carols, and I shall no doubt doze off, as I am prone to do these days, and then I shall wake and muse – muse no doubt about Christmases past, as they were told to me by my mother; as she said they were long before I was born, at the beginning, or should I say at the end, of the world? If I sleep through the night in the Christmas Room, I will probably awake in the morning to the very different music of the minarets which no town or city is now without, as the Faithful are called to prayer and the Infidels are chastised.

I shall take the notebook with the blue cover with me to the Christmas Room, and I shall dip into it there, perhaps between carols. Somehow, and I'm not completely sure why, I feel the Christmas Room and the notebook with the blue cover were made for each other. Whether they were made for me or I for them is a question that must be left unanswered – at least, by me.

21
The Mirror Man

My resolve to enjoy Christmas in the way described by my mother, despite the public aura of indifference or the growing hostility which now threatened to replace it, was strengthened by a remarkable event that occurred in my late twenties – something that turned out to be the oddest encounter of my life.

It was mid-January, and the snow, turned to grey slush in the city streets, still lay thick on the fields and hills thereabouts. I took it into my head to drive to a place where the highway sprouts smaller branches and the latter give way to small country lanes; I parked at the top of such a lane and started my walk across the fields in the silence that snow seems to bring with it on fields and hills in the absence of howling winds.

I walked across a field, and then another which inclined upward, intrigued by the crunch of my footfalls on the virgin snow, and, as I walked, I began to shiver with the intense cold. This second field rose upwards towards a clump of trees over which rose wisps of smoke. These trees whose branches dripped snow reminded me of the scenes depicted on the Christmas cards my mother showed me, when it was the custom to send them to relatives and friends. Before reaching the trees, I stopped, and decided that enough was enough – I would begin my descent, return to my car, and then to the warming familiarity of home. But, as I turned, a voice, cultured and uncommonly grammatical, rang out, 'And whom do I have the pleasure of addressing?' I turned again. The voice belonged to an elderly man in a hooded jacket, his beard short and grey, his eyes piercingly blue, his face deeply lined. He stood in front of the trees, his legs apart and hands on hips, rather in a posture of defiance. Rather comic, I thought. I hesitated, in a state of shock exacerbated by the cold. 'Well, alright,' he went on, 'and you don't need to know who I am, either.' He turned to walk away, and turned again, 'You could do with a hot cup of tea by the look of you – I've some brewing – I live just back there,' he mentioned nonchalantly with his hand. 'No? Well, please yourself!' With that, he turned again and disappeared into the trees from which, after a moment, I heard a door open and bang shut.

Ignoring the voice of common sense to head back down the field and back to my car, something pinned me to the spot and then drove me forward towards the trees, and I found myself knocking on the door of a wood cabin. 'Changed your mind? Well, the offer still stands,' said the old fellow, stepping aside to let me in. 'Yes, go on, right inside. I suppose I'd better put more wood on the fire. Sit down, if you can find somewhere to sit.' And while he busied himself with the wood-stove, I took in my surroundings. I was in what I took to be the living room, if I may call it that, of a small, sturdily built log cabin; there was an off-room, which perhaps was a bedroom, and I had noticed a small outbuilding on my approach. Amongst the general clutter of books and papers, cups, a whisky bottle or two, ashtrays and pipe-racks, were a small table and two small armchairs, and that seemed to be everything, apart from the wood-stove, which was the focal point. Two small windows looked out onto the winter scene – but there were no curtains, as I recall; nor can I remember any carpets or rugs – but I may be wrong about that.

We sat, sipping hot mugs of sweet tea.

'You're a young man of very few words. Very unusual,' he remarked.

'Well, I prefer to listen,' I found myself saying, after a pause.

His kindly, wrinkled face was freed from the hood, as he divested himself of his jacket and placed it behind him on the chair. 'Very wise.

Very wise. People should listen a lot more and chatter a lot less. Of course, the trick is to listen to the right stuff and disregard the rest. But that's one they haven't yet learned – and probably never *will*!' As if to add weight to the point, he leaned forward in his chair and wagged a finger in my direction; the last word was pronounced with the vigour with which an impatient and not altogether competent carpenter might hit a reluctant nail, smashing it on its head with a vengeance.

I couldn't help smiling, and he couldn't help noticing.

'You might think *me* amusing, young man. But I can tell you a story which would amuse you a great deal more. Oh, yes, a real scream!' With that, he took a small pipe from the pocket of the jacket behind him, lit it with a match, and smoke began to fill the room at once. The whole thing took me aback. I mean, I had heard of such things, things which belonged to a time well before my own, but to actually experience it, to actually see someone smoking a pipe, was quite something. I coughed.

'Oh, does my pipe offend you? I know it's not the thing these days, not the thing at all. But, you see, my cabin is my private place, and I'm free here. These days all places are public and private places have been abolished – yes, yes, I know. The phrase "a private place" has become a contradiction in terms, hasn't it? Yes. So it follows that "a public place" is a tautology. Do you know what "tautology" means? Well, no matter. The point is, you can rest assured that my little cabin is my private place, and pipe smoking is definitely allowed here, unless …'

'No, not at all!' I had coughed again but was in no mood to plead my case. 'You said something about a story – you could tell me a funny story.'

'A *funny* story? Well, I'm not at all sure it's a funny story, no, not sure at all. I said it would *amuse* you – and that's different. Want to hear it?'

'Please,' I nodded.

'It's about the mirror man, that's what I call him. Now, this man used to stand in front of a long mirror, making speeches to an imaginary audience, and, you know, he'd become quite animated, really animated, because he felt so passionate about everything, intensely passionate. Do you know what it is to feel intensely passionate? Well, anyway, he would rant and rave about his favourite subject, and his favourite subject was his *only* subject – in a phrase, man's inhumanity to man. Yes, man's inhumanity to man, in all its many guises: from the cruel husband to the hardened despot, from the lazy official to the incompetent medic, from the heartless taxman to oppressive governments, from indifference to suffering and poverty to the insanity of war. Oh, he had a lot to say about war – "legalised murder" he called it. Now, I ask you, was he mad? Eccentric, certainly, yes? Yes. I suppose you might say he was a comic figure of a man – but I see you're not smiling.'

'It must be difficult for a man like that to endure long in a world like this,' I ventured.

'Ah, now there you have it! I knew this little story wouldn't be wasted on you! I just *knew* it!' he beamed. 'Well, our mirror man would end each of his little tirades with the same litany: "Ladies and Gentlemen," he would say, "that's how I see it, because that's exactly how it is. Legalised crime is the order of the day, the name of the game. Take my advice and have as little as possible to do with politicians and lawyers, and teachers who are incapable of learning anything themselves. Ladies and Gentlemen, I bid you good day!" And the litany would end with a little bow to all the ethereal faces that he might have imagined.'

'What happened to him?' I asked.

'What happened? Well, he died, of course, as we all must. Of natural causes. In fact, it might be said that he died twice, once of natural causes, and before that when he smashed the mirror. Oh, yes! One day he became so irate, he smashed it into fragments. And, then, he had no one to address – not even himself, no one imagined or otherwise. Perhaps he died in just that moment – or a part of him died. Hard to say. Perhaps he felt hard done-by. But since he had been addressing only an imaginary audience, he could hardly have expected to receive any merit at all. But then, he clearly hadn't expected much from a real audience, either – otherwise why talk into the mirror at all? He knew full well that praise is never forthcoming from those, and their number is legion, who believe that, in giving it, they are somehow diminishing themselves. And he knew that a prophet is without honour in his own country. And, after all, it was *his* country, *his* world, at which he threw all his abuse. You see, he was himself part of all that was the subject of his own invective. His problem was man's inhumanity to man, and he was himself a man – on the giving as well as the receiving end of all he loathed. Perhaps he had begun to distrust himself, despise himself, even. Hard to say. Hard to say.'

'I still don't get it,' I said, after a long pause. 'Why did he break the mirror?'

'That, young man, is a question to occupy your vacant hours – a lifelong curiosity, perhaps.'

With that, the old fellow pulled his chair closer to the wood-stove and re-lit his pipe, lighting a nearby candle at the same, for the light was beginning to fade on that short, winter day, and the shadows were deepening.

We both sat in silence, serenaded by the crackling, spluttering fire and the gentle sound of puffing as the old fellow returned to his pipe. The silence and the growing shadows in the room were not at all unsettling or discomforting. On the contrary, the fire was the focal point of our gaze, the reddened wood slowly disintegrating before our eyes, the flames darting in and out from crevices that resembled caves in the bowels of the earth, the whole thing a red planet on a course of steady and inevitable destruction, with the ebb and flow of red-yellow flame, all in a constant state of flux, until nothing would be left save the grey ash, an amalgam of what were once living things, tall and masterful in the woodlands. The thought occurred to me that the old fellow was also the product of change, as I have become better to know, and that his life was quickly turning full circle. There were questions I asked in my own mind and dared not ask him, I think because it seemed inappropriate, offensive even, to break the dark and smoky silence with what he might take to be idle curiosity. Had he lived here all his life? Surely not. Was he once a small boy running helter-skelter among those same trees that shielded the cabin? What would the answer matter? And if the answer mattered little, so did the question.

I noticed he had stopped puffing on his pipe, which, now extinguished, rested smokeless in his hand.

It was time to leave. Rising carefully so as not to disturb what I took to be his slumbers, I made for the door. On reaching it, he spoke without stirring from his armchair, and his words have haunted me ever since. 'Remember, now! There are no happy endings to the stories of our lives. If we can find no happiness at all before the end, we are indeed wretched creatures all. Oh, there are pleasures to be had, but no amount of pleasure can give you happiness – it's not even second best. A curse, then, on all those who, through sheer ignorance, gross error of judgement, a sense of misguided benevolence, or the stark mentality of the brute, make happiness for the rest of us an impossible dream. Goodbye!' He uttered this last sentence slowly and deliberately. It occurred to me later how well-formed, measured and intoned his sentence was, as though he had been at great pains to avoid the errors and ambiguities that speed or careless syntax might engender. He reminded me of what I'd read about someone called Percy, in the notebook with the blue cover. A Percy come to life again, as though unwilling to lie motionless in eternal rest, and as restless as dry leaves in the harsh winds of winter.

His farewell turned out to be permanent, for we were never to meet again. As for the cabin, at first I saw it abandoned, with door and windows boarded up, and then, some time later, it was thoroughly dilapidated, a crumbling ruin, hardly one wall standing intact. At times, I have imagined that it was all a dream – that I had dreamed it all. But no dream could leave such a clear and lasting impression.